"Actually, we will be more than friends, Cassandra."

"More than friends?"

Antonio laughed. "Didn't we agree to be colleagues in a friendly little conspiracy...?"

"Oh, you mean our parents. Of course!" She raised her water glass. "To your mother and my father...and whatever the future may bring."

Even as Cassandra and Antonio toasted their harmless matchmaking scheme, she had an unsettling feeling in the pit of her stomach. What was it? What was her heart trying to tell her? She had no words for it, but she sensed she was opening the door to a barrage of emotional complications she had never bargained for. And now, as Antonio clasped her hand across the table, she knew it was too late to turn back....

Books by Carole Gift Page

Love Inspired

In Search of Her Own #4
Decidedly Married #22
Rachel's Hope #40
A Family To Cherish #88
Cassandra's Song #141

CAROLE GIFT PAGE

writes from the heart about issues facing women today. A prolific author of over forty books and 800 stories and articles, she has published both fiction and nonfiction with a dozen major Christian publishers, including Thomas Nelson, Moody Press, Crossway Books, Bethany House, Tyndale House and Harvest House. An award-winning novelist, Carole has received the C.S. Lewis Honor Book Award and been a finalist several times for the prestigious Gold Medallion Award and the Campus Life Book of the Year Award.

A frequent speaker at churches, conferences, conventions, schools and retreats around the country, Carole shares her testimony and encourages women everywhere to discover and share their deepest passions, to keep passion alive on the home front and to unleash their passion for Christ (based on her inspiring new book, *Becoming a Woman of Passion,* by Fleming Revell).

Born and raised in Jackson, Michigan, Carole taught creative writing at Biola University in La Mirada, California, and serves on the Advisory Board of the American Christian Writers. She and her husband, Bill, live in Southern California and have three children (besides Misty in heaven) and three beautiful grandchildren.

Cassandra's Song
Carole Gift Page

Published by Steeple Hill Books™

STEEPLE HILL BOOKS

ISBN 0-373-87148-1

CASSANDRA'S SONG

But God—so rich is He in His mercy! Because of and in order to satisfy the great and wonderful and intense love with which He loved us, even when we were dead (slain) by [our own] shortcomings and trespasses, He made us alive together in fellowship and in union with Christ; [He gave us the very life of Christ Himself, the same new life with which He quickened Him, for] it is by grace (His favor and mercy which you did not deserve) that you are saved (delivered from judgment and made partakers of Christ's salvation).

—*Ephesians* 2: 4-5

In loving memory of my mother- and father-in-law, Alice and Anthony Page (born Antonio Pagliarulo) and in loving memory of their granddaughter and my niece, Karen Geston Abeloe. Your family loves you and misses you deeply.

Chapter One

Andrew Rowlands was just changing into something comfortable when his oldest daughter Cassandra peeked inside the bedroom door and said, "Dinner will be ready in half an hour, Daddy."

He turned and flashed a generous smile. "Thanks, Cassie. I'll be right down."

She didn't budge, just kept watching him. Her lovely face was doing the thing it always did when she was displeased. Her clear blue eyes darkened, her finely arched brows furrowed, and her heart-shaped lips slipped into a pout. "Oh, Daddy!"

"What's wrong, kitten?" It was all he could do to hold back a chuckle. Cassie was twenty-six years old, but that childlike scowl brought back memories of a strong-willed toddler who stubbornly held her ground when she wanted something. How often he and Mandy had exchanged helpless smiles when their daughter folded her chubby arms and crooned, "Please, Mommy... Please, Daddy!"

"So what's up, honey?" he asked now. "You look like you have something to say."

She shook her pretty blond head. "No, Daddy. It's just... you're not going to wear that ratty old sweater to dinner, are you?"

He glanced in the mirror at his rumpled, brown, button-down sweater. "Why not? It's my favorite. I've worn it all my life."

"I know, Daddy. It looks it! Why don't you wear your new dress shirt and the tie I gave you last Christmas?"

"For Pete's sake, I'm only going downstairs to my own dining room for a heaping plate of spaghetti." Fridays were always spaghetti nights. His youngest daughter Frannie's specialty. She had become chief cook and bottle washer after Mandy's death five years ago. A downright good cook she had become, too. Of his three daughters Frannie was most like her mother—a charming little spitfire at heart and oh, so overly protective. As if he needed protecting at his age!

"So will you change, Daddy?" Cassie remained in the doorway, grilling him with her gaze.

"If you insist. But a good white shirt and spaghetti don't mix well. You know that, especially on laundry days."

She beamed. "Don't worry, Daddy. You won't spill a drop."

He returned a wry smile. "And if you believe that, my beauty, you're sadly deluded. I'll need a bib the size of a pup tent."

Brianna, his middle daughter, had actually stitched

a humongous terry cloth bib for him once—and later made them for her sisters as well—and all his daughters had laughed in bemused delight as she tied it around his neck while he sat, fork and knife ready, to attack a luscious mountain of meatballs and spaghetti. He had smugly devoured the entire plate without so much as a dollop of sauce on that voluminous bib. He had even managed to slip a meatball or two under the table to Ruggs, the family's mop-haired mongrel mascot, so named because as a puppy he had a penchant for burrowing like a gopher under the throw rugs.

Cassie ignored his comment about the bib. "Splash on some of that smelly aftershave, too, Daddy," she urged.

Before he could protest, she slipped back out and shut the door. He scowled at his reflection in the mirror and mumbled, "Something's brewing. Something's always going on with those three girls. Wonder what—or *who*—it is this time?"

In deference to his daughters' wishes—when had he not given in to his daughters?—Andrew reluctantly pulled off his comfy threadbare sweater. With a sigh of resignation he slipped on his starched dress shirt and grabbed the monogrammed silk tie Cassandra had given him last Christmas. He buttoned the shirt and knotted the tie with deft fingers, casting a squint-eyed glance in the dresser mirror at his hefty, six-foot-four frame. Not bad for an old geezer two years short of the half-century mark. He still had his college-football physique in spite of the mountains of spaghetti his daughters had plied him with over the past five years. They hadn't let him miss a meal, that was for sure. Yes, indeed, they were good girls. The best.

He gazed at the familiar framed photograph of his wife on the bureau. "You'd be proud of your daughters, Mandy," he said in a husky whisper, his eyes misting over. "They've taken good care of me since…since we lost you. Too good. I think they're matchmaking again. But they should know they'll never find a woman for me as perfect as their mother."

A familiar ache rose in his chest. After all this time he still felt a compulsive need to confide all the details of his life to his wife, God rest her soul. He cleared his throat and said aloud, "Mandy, I promise you, I'm as determined to protect our daughters, as they are to find me a new wife."

He paused, casting a glance around the comfortable bedroom that had been his and Mandy's for well over twenty years. He hadn't changed a thing since her death—not the chintz curtains or flowered wallpaper or blown-glass knickknacks. Even her perfume decanters remained on the dresser where he could breathe in her scent when he was lonely.

"Truth is, Mandy," he said with a weary sigh, "I'm worried about the girls. They should all be out finding themselves husbands—good, decent, godly men—instead of hanging around the house taking care of me. Sure, they've got busy lives and successful careers, but I want them to experience the kind of love you and I shared. A special devotion only God can give a man and a woman. But, short of my prayers, I haven't a clue how to make sure they find that kind of love.''

Andrew ran a comb through his thick, wavy brown hair and, as Cassie requested, splashed some after-shave on his cheeks. He chuckled craftily. ''This stuff makes me smell like a perfume factory. Just hope the lady they've invited for dinner isn't allergic.''

With a jaunty flourish he straightened his tie and strode out of the room, his head up, shoulders squared. Time to face the music. Or whatever mystery woman the girls had planned for him tonight. He cast a glance heavenward and smiled. *Lord, let this evening not be a total fiasco. I'm sure the girls have worked hard and have the best of intentions. But You know I'm not in the market for a wife, no matter how many socks she can mend or how many soufflés she can bake without collapsing.*

He was halfway down the spiral oak staircase, the pungent aroma of well-done roast beef in his nostrils—what happened to the usual spaghetti?—when he heard the melodic voices of his daughters rising from the kitchen. He paused with a bemused smile and listened. *Let's just see what you girls are up to.*

Cassandra was shouting into the sunroom just off the kitchen. ''Frannie, we need your help! When are you going to finish heaping clay on that monstrosity of a sculpture and come rescue this dinner?''

Frannie, from the sunroom: ''It's not a monstrosity; it's a bust of Amelia Earhart, and if I stop now the clay will harden.''

''But you're the cook in the family,'' Brianna, his

middle child, protested. "Just come check the roast, Frannie. Please! It's tough as leather. What can we do with it?"

"Play football," came the miffed retort.

"Good one, Frannie," said Andrew under his breath from his stairway perch. He laughed in spite of himself. "My mellow, dulcet daughters. The three muses. Should have named them Faith, Hope and Love."

At the moment their mellifluous voices were rising in shrill desperation. "Frannie, get in here! Bree is scorching the roast!"

"Not me, Frannie. It's Cassie."

"Okay, I'm coming. Just give me a minute," said Frannie, sounding exasperated. "But if the dinner is wrecked, that's what you two get for trying to marry Daddy off to every unattached woman in town!"

Andrew meandered on down the stairs. He couldn't stifle another smile. Maybe the humiliation of a burned roast would teach his daughters to lay off the matchmaking. He sauntered into the kitchen where he could see Frannie in the sunroom beside the armature of her latest sculpture; she was in her artist's smock, wet clay up to her elbows. Cassandra and Brianna stood beside the kitchen stove, peering into a pan that contained a black mound that could have been a large lump of coal or a small meteor that had burned up on entering earth's atmosphere.

"Daddy, there's a little problem with dinner," Bree said. "I was on the phone with a client whose husband ran off with his secretary and left her alone with seven children. She was so upset, I just couldn't break away—"

"And, Daddy, I was in the music room practicing the piano for Sunday's cantata," Cassandra lamented, "and it never occurred to me a roast needed so much water—"

"That's because you two leave all the cooking to me," Frannie said, emerging from the sunroom brushing a wisp of golden hair back from her clay-smudged cheek.

"That's because we both work and you're here at home...sculpting," Cassandra stated thickly. "Besides, you always say you love cooking for Daddy."

"I do, and if I'd had my way, we'd be having our usual spaghetti. It's Daddy's favorite." She looked petulantly at Andrew. "Isn't it, Daddy?"

"Yes, dear, but I love anything my girls fix, you know that."

"Even this burnt offering?" challenged Frannie, pointing a clay-caked finger accusingly at the charred roast.

Andrew grimaced. A layer of smoke had settled around the ceiling, and he had to admit the smell was slightly reminiscent of brimstone. "Well, it's the...the thought that counts. But maybe tonight we might think about going out to dinner." He flicked his starched collar. "After all, I'm already dressed up."

"That's not necessary, Daddy," said Frannie, going to the sink and turning on the spigot. "I'll wash up and fix my usual spaghetti." She gave her sisters a knowing look. "I should have it ready by the time our guest arrives."

"Guest?" echoed Andrew, feigning ignorance.

Brianna tossed back her long russet hair, her cheeks turning a deep rose. "We're having company, Daddy. Hope you don't mind."

"Mind? Why would I mind?" He could play their little game. "Who's coming to dinner? Someone I know?"

"No, Daddy," Cassandra said, nervously patting her upswept chignon. Several ringlets of her silky champagne-blond hair bobbed against her high cheekbones as she placed the lid on the roast and carried the pan toward the back door. "I'll just put this outside where it can't hurt anyone, and be right back."

"Don't feed it to Ruggs," warned Frannie. "We don't want to have to rush him off to the vet tonight."

"Don't worry, sister dear. I'll dispose of this culinary disaster in the garbage. You just get that spaghetti started."

"You girls still haven't told me. Who's coming over?"

Bree averted her gaze. "A very nice lady from my counseling center. She's a child psychologist. We work together sometimes when I'm counseling families going through death or divorce. She's wonderful with troubled children. You'll love her, Daddy."

"What's her name?" asked Andrew, maintaining a noncommittal tone.

Brianna flashed a beatific smile. "Emma Sorenson."

"Emma Sorenson?" countered Cassandra, returning inside from the backyard with Ruggs yapping at her heels. The roly-poly, mop-faced animal, probably a hundred in dog years, leaped up eagerly on Andrew, his big paws leaving grimy prints on Andrew's dress shirt.

"Okay, Ruggsy, boy, that's enough. Down, boy!"

"What do you mean, Emma Sorenson!" Cassandra repeated, staring Brianna down. "My dear sister, we were supposed to invite Lydia Dibbles, that new lady in church."

Bree stared back, refusing to be intimidated. "I called Lydia and she wasn't home, so I asked Emma at work the next day."

"Well, I saw Lydia at church on Sunday and invited her!" Cassandra's voice had reached a decibel level that would have amazed even her music teachers at Juilliard.

There was dead silence as everyone recognized their awkward dilemma. Andrew broke the silence good-naturedly commenting, "Ah, now I see. We're expecting *two* dinner guests. Marvelous. I'll put another chair around the table."

Chapter Two

Cassandra moaned in surprise as the doorbell rang. "Oh, no! I'll get it, but it's too late to 'uninvite' anybody. Bree, hurry and put another place setting on the table. Frannie, turn up the burner under the spaghetti. And, Daddy, get that smirk off your face. This isn't funny."

Andrew held up his hands placatingly, but there was an unmistakable gleam in his eyes. "I'm innocent in this little caper. But you know what they say, girls. The more the merrier."

Brianna shook her head in mock despair. "Oh, this is going to be a fun evening. I can see it already."

"Just keep smiling, girls, no matter what happens!" With that lame bit of advice, Cassandra turned on her stacked heels and strode down the hall to the wide marble entry. She wiped her moist palms on the ruffled apron that covered her knit, lime-green dress, then flung open the double doors with a welcoming smile in place.

Lydia Dibbles, an attractive fortyish matron in a smart pale-blue leisure suit, stood on the sprawling, lattice-trimmed porch. She was a short, buxom woman with bright, violet eyes, a generous smile in her round face, and silver streaks in her auburn hair.

"Lydia, welcome," Cassandra said with a little too much relief in her voice. Maybe the other woman wouldn't show up after all and they would be saved the embarrassment of this doomed "double date." "Come in, please come in."

Lydia stepped inside. "Thank you, Cassie. My, you look pretty tonight. Your cheeks are red as roses. I bet you've been slaving over a hot stove all day."

"You could say that. May I, um, take your coat?"

Lydia shrugged. "I don't have a coat, dear."

Cassie laughed self-consciously. "Of course you don't." She was about to shut the double doors when she spied another figure in a gray pantsuit coming up the walk...a tall, slender woman with a brown pageboy and wire-rim glasses.

"Emma? Emma Sorenson?" Cassie asked as the woman scaled the porch steps.

"Yes, I'm Emma. And you must be Brianna's sister."

"Yes, I'm Cassie, the oldest." She beckoned Emma inside. "I'm so glad you could come to dinner, Emma." Cassie looked apprehensively over at Lydia and added, "*Both* of you."

The two women gazed at each other and exchanged polite but curious smiles.

"Emma, this is Lydia," Cassie said brightly. "Lydia, Emma."

"Goodness, I didn't realize this was going to be a party," said Lydia, looking mildly flustered.

"Just a small dinner party," Cassie assured her. "Come with me, ladies."

"You have a lovely home," Emma stated, gazing around as they passed through the parlor to the dining room. "Such a stately old house. I bet it has a wonderful history."

Cassie chuckled and said under her breath, "Oh, yes, we're making history in this house all the time."

As they entered the dining room, her father came to her rescue, bounding toward their visitors as if *two* guests had been the operative number all along.

"Well, ladies, welcome! I'm so glad you could join us for dinner."

"Thank you, Reverend Rowlands," Lydia said shyly. "I've so enjoyed your messages. You have a wonderful way of speaking. I always leave church feeling blessed."

"Well, thank you kindly. You've certainly made my day."

"Daddy, this is Lydia Dibbles," said Cassie. "And this is Emma..."

"Sorenson. Your daughter Brianna and I work together at the family counseling center, Reverend Rowlands. She has a heart of pure gold, that girl. Folks love her."

"Yes, she has a real heart for people," said Andrew, leading the two women toward the linen-draped table. "And, please, both of you call me Andrew. The title *Reverend* intimidates even me."

Lydia twittered, "Oh, Andrew, what a precious sense of humor you have!"

While her father kept their two guests entertained, Cassandra excused herself and headed for the kitchen. "Is the salad ready, Bree? Let's get this dinner over with before everything blows up in our faces."

Bree tossed the salad greens. "Let's not panic. Maybe Daddy won't mind having two dates."

"Are you kidding?" countered Frannie as she drained the pasta. "Until a few minutes ago he didn't even know he was having one date! If you two keep up your matchmaking schemes, Daddy will banish the three of us from this house."

Cassandra stared skeptically at her youngest sister. "Why on earth would he do that? He loves having us here. We're all he has."

"And all he needs," Frannie said. "Daddy's perfectly happy with things just the way they are, so why shouldn't we be, too?"

Brianna placed silver tongs in the salad bowl. "But we've got to be realistic, Frannie. Someday the three of us will want lives of our own. We'll get married and move away. Then who will take care of Daddy?"

"Move away? Speak for yourself," Frannie said. "I have no plans to leave home. I like it here. I like taking care of Daddy."

"We all do," conceded Cassie. "We have a wonderful family. I don't know of any family as close as we are. But, still, someday one of us might meet someone and decide to…to get married."

"Bite your tongue," said Frannie with a grudging little smile. "I'm only twenty-two and I've still got to establish my reputation as a serious artist."

Bree nodded. "I know, but I'm already twenty-four and wouldn't mind meeting the right man. And with Cassie twenty-six, she'll need to start thinking about her biological clock one of these days."

"My biological clock?" Cassie exclaimed with mock indignation. "We're talking about Daddy here, not me. And my biological clock is doing just fine, thank you."

"I didn't mean anything negative," Bree assured her. "It's just that you might want to start thinking about having a home and family of your own."

Cassie put her hands on her hips and stared hard at her sister. "So what is it, Bree? Now I'm an old maid needing a man to make me feel fulfilled? That concept went out in the last century!"

Bree stared right back. "For heaven's sake, Cassie, I'm just trying to make Frannie understand why we're trying to find the right woman for Dad. Then any one of us can feel free to get married or travel or whatever. We won't have to feel guilty about leaving Daddy to shift for himself."

"Well, you two can go if you want to," Frannie said with a determined little pout, "but I'm staying right here. Nothing could make me leave."

"I'm not planning to leave either," Cassie agreed. "I have my music, and I'm not about to let any man distract me from becoming a concert pianist. So there."

"Well, I'm not leaving, either," Bree said. "Besides, where would we find a woman who deserved our dad?''

"Fine," Frannie huffed. "So let's serve dinner and send our guests on their way."

For the first few minutes, dinner went well. Brianna served the salad, Cassie the garlic bread and Frannie the spaghetti. The conversation around the table was polite, if a bit reserved. Then their father asked the question Cassie was dreading.

"Where are our bibs, Bree?"

"Bibs?" repeated Lydia Dibbles, mystified.

"Bibs?" echoed Emma Sorenson, her penciled brows rising.

"Yes, bibs," Andrew stated as if his meaning were obvious. "We can't eat spaghetti without bibs." He smiled patiently at Emma and Lydia. "Brianna made us these gargantuan bibs that keep the tomato sauce off our clothes. She started with one for me." He speared a meatball and held it up, red sauce dripping from the fork's tines. "As you can see, I'm clumsy as they come."

"A bib for adults! What a clever idea," Lydia said.

Andrew nodded. "Exactly! And soon we were all using them. They free you up to slurp your spaghetti strands, if that happens to be your thing. I never could get the hang of twirling spaghetti on my fork."

"Daddy," Cassandra interrupted sharply, "I'm sure our guests don't want to wear bibs. Bibs are for babies, toddlers..."

"Nonsense! Why wouldn't they want to protect those lovely outfits?" With a twinkle in his eyes Andrew jumped up from the table, strode to the buffet and removed what appeared to be a stack of white terry cloth towels.

Cassie lowered her gaze and shook her head as her father tied a bib first around Emma's neck and then Lydia's. He went on to fasten a bib around each daughter's neck, planting a kiss on the tops of their heads, and finally he tied a bib around his own neck and sat down, looking quite pleased with himself.

The women seemed dumbstruck at first as they gazed down at their enormous bibs, but then they began to giggle, and soon everyone in the room was laughing uproariously and making outrageous jokes.

"If we were wearing black, we'd look like penguins," Emma said with a chuckle.

"I could wear this to the beauty shop when I have my hair done. It's certainly large enough," Lydia observed.

"Have you thought of going into business, Andrew?" suggested Emma. "Marketing bibs for adults. I'm sure it's a fad many of us would welcome. You could personalize them. Oh, there's no end to what you could do. Cover them with pictures, make them in bright colors..."

"What a wonderful idea, Emma," said Lydia. "I may try my hand at a few myself. I know several little craft stores that might welcome them."

"I wouldn't mind working with you, Lydia. I have a sewing machine and have been known to be quite a seamstress in my time."

"Oh, that might be fun, dear. What do you think,

Andrew? Would you mind us taking your idea and running with it?''

''No, of course not, although maybe you should check with Bree. It was her idea in the first place.''

''No, that's fine,'' Brianna said quickly. ''I'd love to see what the two of you come up with.''

When everyone had finished their spaghetti, Cassie served coffee and Frannie brought out her special strawberry shortcake for dessert. It was obviously a favorite of everyone's.

When at last dinner was finished, Cassie breathed a little sigh of relief. Considering the catastrophe she had expected this evening to be, everything had gone amazingly well. Lydia and Emma were already behaving like long-lost friends, and her father seemed to be genuinely enjoying the company of his two dates. But now that dinner was over she wanted to send them on their way before she pushed her good fortune too far.

''Well, it's been wonderful having you both here,'' she told her two guests as she collected the dessert plates. It's just too bad we have to make it an early evening. Daddy has to work on his sermon tonight, you know.''

''Oh, yes, Daddy,'' Frannie chimed in, ''don't forget your sermon. You must still have hours of research to do.''

Her father looked from daughter to daughter with a question mark in his eyes. ''My sermon?'' He broke into a self-satisfied grin. ''Actually, my sermon is done. I'm as ready for Sunday as I'll ever be.''

''But, Daddy, you can't be,'' protested Frannie.

"Oh, but I am, muffin." He grinned slyly. "I'm speaking on the importance of letting God do His work in our lives rather than trying to orchestrate the future ourselves. After all, we end up in quite a pickle when we try to—"

"Yes, Daddy, we get the message," Cassie said, sweeping over and helping her father take off his bib. "I'll collect the bibs, and then we can...we can, uh..."

Her father broke in. "Why don't we adjourn to the music room and let Cassie give us a preview of Sunday's cantata?"

"Oh, that would be delightful," said Emma.

"No, Daddy, I really couldn't tonight."

Andrew wasn't about to be deterred. "Well, then let's gather around the piano and have an old-fashioned hymn sing. How about it, ladies?"

Emma clapped her hands. "Oh, I love to sing. What about you, Lydia?"

"I'm not much of a singer, but I'll give it the old college try."

Brianna and Frannie cast sidelong glances at Cassie, as if to ask, Now what do we do? Cassie shrugged helplessly, her arms filled with bibs. Nothing about this evening was going the way she had expected.

Her father gave a contented sigh. "Good dinner, girls. You outdid yourselves as usual." He pushed back his chair and stood, then helped Emma and Lydia out of their chairs. As he motioned the women toward the music room, he tweaked Cassie's cheek and said, "You'll come play for us, won't you, cupcake?"

Her shoulders sagged. "Sure, Daddy, I'll be right there."

"And Bree and Frannie, you'll join us, too, won't you?" her father urged. "You girls have such lovely voices."

"Sure, Daddy," they said in unison.

For the next two hours they sat around the piano singing every hymn they could recall, Cassie's tapered fingers moving expertly over the ivory keys as her father's rich baritone blended with his daughters' lyrical sopranos and the eager, if unpracticed, altos of their two guests.

At some point Cassie lost track of time and realized, to her surprise, that she was thoroughly enjoying the evening. In fact, it was obvious that everyone was having a marvelous time, especially her father and his impromptu dates.

It was nearly midnight when Lydia and Emma said their reluctant good-nights, "Dear girls, we must do this again very soon! Your father is such a treasure! You must be so proud!" and slipped off into the night, chatting amiably, as if they had known each other forever.

With the ladies gone, Andrew beckoned his daughters close and drew them into what might have been a football huddle, his arms draped around their shoulders, their heads all nearly touching at the forehead. "My darling daughters," he said in a soft, wily voice, "I know you love practicing your matchmaking schemes on me, but setting me up with two dates in one night? Isn't that a bit much even for you?''

"Oh, Daddy, we didn't mean to," Brianna exclaimed. "I invited Emma—"

"And I invited Lydia," Cassie said. "I didn't know about Emma until—"

"Well, girls, next time coordinate your efforts, okay?" Andrew's expression grew solemn, the sea-blue of his eyes deepening. "In fact, I would prefer that there be no more matchmaking efforts on my behalf. Is that understood?"

"But, Daddy," protested Cassie.

"No buts, Cassie. I'm very happy with my life just as it is." An unexpected tenderness softened his voice. "I had a wonderful life with your mother. She was the love of my life, and I don't expect to find another woman I could love that way again. So, please, promise me, no more conniving to get me to the altar again. Promise?"

"Promise, Daddy," Frannie agreed.

Brianna looked reluctant, but finally acquiesced. "Promise."

Cassie turned away, silent. There was no way she could make such a promise. She knew what her father needed even if he didn't...an extraordinary woman who would love him with the kind of passion and devotion that would erase the grief and loneliness she saw in his eyes when he thought nobody was looking.

Somewhere in this vast, wide world there had to be such a woman.

Chapter Three

On Saturday morning—a balmy, early autumn day—Frannie poked her head inside Cassie's door and whispered, "You awake, sleepyhead?"

Cassie rolled over and burrowed her head under the pillow. "No, go away. After last night's fiasco, I want to sleep till noon!"

Frannie slipped inside the room and curled up on a corner of the four-poster bed. "It wasn't so bad. We actually had fun, didn't we? And Dad was a good sport, don't you think? So it all turned out okay. As long as we don't try playing matchmaker again."

Cassie pulled her tousled head out from under the pillow and looked at her youngest sister through bleary eyes. Frannie was sitting cross-legged in her PJs, her golden hair cascading over her shoulders to the middle of her back. "Fran, did you wake me up just to rehash last night?"

"Of course not."

"We're not having more dinner guests tonight, are we?"

"No. Not at all."

"Good!"

"But I, uh, have a favor to ask."

Cassie fluffed her pillow under her head and closed her eyes. "Your timing is lousy, sis. Whatever it is, no!"

"Then you won't go?" Frannie's tone was petulant.

Cassie opened one eye, her curiosity rising in spite of herself. "Go where?"

"To the concert tonight."

"What concert?"

"At the university."

"San Diego State?"

"Of course. What other school is there?" Frannie drew in a breath and rushed on. "Antonio Pagliarulo is performing."

Cassie sat up and forked back her mop of unruly hair. "Who?" she asked, feigning ignorance.

"Antonio Pagliarulo. A fantastic tenor. He teaches music at the university. You teach in the music department. Surely you know him."

"I'm part-time faculty. I go, teach my two classes, and disappear again. Full-timers don't mingle with part-timers."

"Well, I'm only a teacher's assistant, and I've heard of Antonio Pagliarulo."

"Okay, so I've heard of him. They say he's a recluse, a loner, a snob. Lives in a mansion overlooking the ocean and never socializes with anyone."

"So?" countered Frannie. "They say he's as handsome and mysterious as an old-time matinee idol and has a voice like Pavarotti."

Cassie swung her long legs over the bed. "Okay, you win. I'll go with you to the concert."

"Oh, I'm not going," said Frannie quickly.

"Not going? You just invited me!"

Frannie's blue eyes flashed. "I want you to go so I can stay home."

Cassie covered her ears. "Oh, no, I don't want to hear this!"

Frannie sat up on her knees and seized Cassie's hand. "Please, sis," she implored, "just do this one favor for me and I'll never ask again. I've got a date to the concert with Gilbert Dooley."

"Gilbert Who-ley?"

"He's very nice. He teaches at the university."

"And I'm to fill in for you? No way. You always come up with some oddball—"

"He's not odd at all. He's a professor, a brain like you, like—"

Cassie managed a teasing smile. "Then what is he doing dating you?"

"We're not dating. It's purely platonic. He teaches physical science. We bump into each other once in a while. He said he got the last two concert tickets, and in a moment of weakness I agreed to go with him."

"Then go."

"I can't. I've got to stay home and finish my sculpture before the clay hardens. If I don't, Amelia Earhart will end up looking like Daffy Duck!"

"Amelia Earhart is dead."

"I know, but I'm bringing her back to life…in clay. Please, Cassie."

Cassie sank back on the bed with a weary sigh. "All right, I'll go. But you owe me, Frannie. You owe me big!"

Later that afternoon, as Cassie swirled her saffron hair into a French twist, she was already sorry she had given in. She had no desire to go on a blind date with anyone, least of all some science professor who would probably talk theorems all evening. Or was that math? Whatever.

Hoping for a look that was simple, elegant and tastefully understated, she slipped into a black crepe dress with a tunic top and ankle-length skirt. Good, it was just the look she wanted—classic but certainly not provocative.

Gilbert Dooley arrived at the stroke of six, as he had promised. After his initial surprise, he seemed to take the date switch with surprising aplomb and civility. Or maybe he was a better actor than Cassie suspected. One thing for sure, he was definitely not Frannie's type. Nor Cassie's! Tall, middle-aged and balding, he was as lean as a windlestraw, with pale-white skin and faded gray eyes behind enormous bifocals.

On the way to the concert hall in Gilbert's antediluvian sedan, he kept up a steady stream of conversation, enlightening her as to the laws of thermodynamics, time dilation and universal gravitation. But he became most impassioned when speaking of his favorite topic, the superconducting supercollider.

"Can you imagine, Cassandra?" he enthused. "It has the potential of being the world's largest particle accelerator. Think of what it will tell us about the Big Bang!"

"I can only imagine," Cassie mumbled. In her mind she was plotting ways she would get back at her youngest sister. She could spike her oatmeal with raisins—she hated the chewy little beasts—or she could tie her socks in knots or put ice cubes in her bed. No, she hadn't pulled those pranks since she was ten. There had to be some suitable, but harmless, pranks for grown-up sisters to play on one another.

Cassie and Gilbert arrived at the concert hall with ample time to spare. She cringed a little when two of her students passed by and rolled their eyes as she and the professor walked down the aisle to their seats. She wanted to call out, He's not my date! I don't even know what I'm doing here!

At least they had good seats, center section, four rows from the stage. Cassie had performed enough concerts of her own that she always felt a heart-pounding excitement when the house lights lowered and a white-hot spotlight carved a luminous circle out of the hushed darkness. It was happening now, the audience din shrinking to silence as the enormous red velvet curtain rose to reveal a lone man on center stage. Dressed in a black tuxedo, he was tall, dark and imposing, his shoulders as broad as his waist was narrow, an aristocratic air in his demeanor.

As the orchestra began to play, Antonio Pagliarulo launched into an Italian aria with the richest, fullest, most enchanting tenor voice Cassie had ever heard.

She sat mesmerized, dazzled, disarmed. No matter what anybody said about this man, he could hold an audience spellbound.

During her two semesters of part-time teaching, Cassie had passed Antonio occasionally on the university campus, but hadn't bothered to give him a second glance in spite of his swarthy good looks. For too many years she had disciplined her mind to concentrate only on her music, her career. Focusing on attractive men would only divert her from her lifelong goals. Besides, she had already been burned once and wasn't about to risk a broken heart again. But now, tonight, she was seeing this talented, enigmatic man with new eyes. She liked what she saw...and was hopelessly enraptured by what she heard.

It seemed only minutes had passed and already Antonio was singing his final number. When the audience gave him a standing ovation, Cassie was one of the first to stand. She applauded until her palms stung. Then, all too soon, it was time to leave.

"There's a reception for Mr. Pagliarulo in the faculty hall, if you'd like to go," Gilbert told her as they made their way out of the crowded auditorium.

"I'd love to," she said without hesitation.

A gentle breeze was rising off the ocean as Gilbert escorted Cassie across the darkened campus to the faculty hall. He held her elbow to keep her from falling, and to her relief was no longer talking about centrifugal force and cold fusion. In fact, he seemed as enthralled by Antonio Pagliarulo's voice as she was. "I rarely go to programs like this," he was saying, "but Tonio has been more than a colleague to me, he's been rather like a confidant. So I promised him I would attend one of his concerts."

"You're saying Antonio Pagliarulo is a good friend of yours?" Cassie asked, hardly hiding her surprise.

Gilbert's countenance grew pink. "I admit, Cassandra, I'm not a very social person, but yes, Tonio's been a good friend to me."

"That's not what I meant. It's just that I'd heard Antonio was a loner, snobbish, reclusive."

"I suppose he is, to most people. But that's not the man I know."

"I...I'd like to meet him."

"Then I'll introduce you."

The faculty hall was brimming with people, most of them converging on Antonio. Cassie shook her head. There was no way to get close.

"Don't worry," said Gilbert. "We'll have some refreshments and wait for the crowd to thin out." He led her over to a row of straight-back chairs lining one end of the hall. "Sit down and relax. I'll get us something to eat."

Taking the closest chair, Cassie sat down and smiled politely at the attractive woman walking toward her. In her mid-forties, she was an exotic beauty, with ebony hair, olive skin, red lips and flashing coal-black eyes. Wearing a stylish red velvet evening dress swishing over rounded hips, she was a startling contradiction of elegance and flamboyance.

The woman flashed a beaming smile as she

pointed to the empty chair beside Cassie. "May I?" she asked with the hint of an accent.

"Please do. I guess we both had the same idea. It'll be a half hour at least before we can get through the crowd to greet Mr. Pagliarulo."

"Oh, I wasn't waiting for the crowds," said the woman. "I just wanted to sit down. I never should have worn these insufferable three-inch heels tonight. Next time I will wear my comfortable bunny slippers. I don't care how silly I look, at least my feet will not be in pain."

Cassie stifled a spurt of laughter. The idea of this sophisticated matron wearing bunny slippers was hilariously implausible.

"You think I am speaking in jest," the woman said, her smile expanding to reveal perfect white teeth. "Watch this." With a little flourish she kicked off her shoes and wriggled her stockinged feet. "See? That is much better. Now I may survive this night. Or do I embarrass you with my lack of manners?"

Cassie chuckled in spite of herself. "Oh, no. I love people who aren't afraid of what other people think."

"Then you are a young lady after my own heart," said the woman, patting Cassie's hand. "My name is Juliana. What is yours?"

"Cassandra. But most people call me Cassie."

"I prefer Cassandra," said Juliana with a little wave of her hand. "It is a regal name. A name for a princess. It fits you well."

Cassie smiled. It was Juliana who looked like a

princess. Better yet, a queen. "I assure you," said Cassie, "I'm no princess."

"But you carry yourself like one. What do you do? Are you in music...theater? I can imagine you onstage."

Cassie felt her cheeks glow. "How did you know?"

"I see it in your face, the way you carry yourself. You are a creative person. I guessed music because you are here at this concert."

"I'm a pianist," said Cassie. "I've performed a few concerts, but nothing as impressive as this. I teach a couple of piano classes here at the university. And I'm the music director at my father's church."

"Your father's church? That is wonderful," said Juliana. "It is good to use one's talents for God."

"Yes, it is."

"I would love to hear you play sometime."

Cassie hesitated. "I—I am playing in a cantata tomorrow night."

"Is it nearby?"

"The Cornerstone Christian Church in La Jolla."

"Oh, that isn't far from here. I might be able to attend."

"That would be wonderful."

But would she really show up? Cassie wondered. People were always promising to get together or do lunch or stop by, but they rarely followed through.

Juliana touched Cassie's arm with graceful, tapered fingers. "You do not believe I will come, do you?"

"Oh, no, I—"

"But I will. I must ask my son. He drives me. I have no sense of direction. I would end up in the ocean on my way to Hawaii instead of La Jolla. So I will ask my son and he will bring me."

"Oh, do come. Both of you," said Cassie. "Bring the rest of your family, too. Your husband—"

"My husband has been dead for many years, so it can only be my son and me."

"I'm sorry," said Cassie quickly. "Listen, I'll write out the directions for your son. The cantata is at 8:00 p.m., but the church will be crowded, so you may want to come around seven." Like a lightning bolt, an idea struck Cassie straight out of the blue, but she recognized it instantly as pure genius. This Juliana was a woman even Cassie's hard-to-please father might find fascinating. No harm in setting something up and seeing what happened.

"Maybe you would like to join my family afterward for a bite to eat," Cassie suggested, her plan already brewing. "I would like you to meet my father…and my sisters, too, of course."

"Your invitation is very generous," said Juliana warmly. "I will ask my son. If he has no prior commitment, we will join you."

"Wonderful," said Cassie with a pleased little smile.

Their conversation broke off as Gilbert returned with two plates of finger sandwiches and cake and paper cups of red punch. He sat down beside Cassie and handed her a plate and cup. "The crowd is thinning out," he noted. "After we eat I'll introduce you to Tonio."

"Fine," she said with a nod, then introduced Gilbert to Juliana. "Gilbert and I will be making our way through the crowd to meet Mr. Pagliarulo. Would you like to join us, Juliana?"

The woman flashed a whimsical smile. "Yes, I may do that. So you have never met Mr. Pagliarulo?"

"I've seen him come and go in the fine arts building, but we haven't met." Cassie lowered her voice confidentially. "I've heard he is something of a recluse. A loner. Not easy to know. Does he strike you as snobbish or arrogant?"

Juliana's eyes sparkled with amusement. "Oh, is that how he seems to you? A snob?"

"No, not really. Not when he was onstage. He was absolutely wonderful. But I've heard others say—"

Juliana wriggled her stockinged feet back into her shoes and stood up with a jaunty shake of her head. "Come! Let us go see if this Antonio Pagliarulo is an arrogant, unsociable man."

Flustered, Cassie handed Gilbert her plate and cup and followed Juliana across the hall. "I didn't mean...Juliana, wait, please." Gilbert caught up with them, dropping the paper plates and cups into a trash receptacle. Juliana briskly carved a path for them through the remaining cluster of fans.

And suddenly Cassie found herself face-to-face with the handsome, mysterious Antonio Pagliarulo. He gazed down at her with shrewd, dark eyes, a smile playing at the curve of his lips. In person, up close, he seemed even more imposing than he had onstage. Larger than life, his very presence was stunning, unnerving. She found herself feeling as tongue-tied as a schoolgirl.

Gilbert spoke up, his voice taking a shrill high note. "Tonio, I'd like you to meet my date, Cassandra Rowlands."

Cassie offered her hand, even though it was trembling and her palm was moist. "Mr. Pagliarulo, I—I enjoyed your performance immensely," she breathed.

He clasped her hand in both of his. His touch was warm, electric, his solemn gaze riveting. "How do you do, Miss Rowlands?"

Cassie turned to Juliana. "Mr. Pagliarulo, I'd like you to meet—"

With a little burst of laughter, Antonio sprang forward and gathered the dark-haired Juliana into his arms. Cassie stared in mute astonishment as the two embraced. "Antonio, you were marvelous this evening," Juliana enthused.

Antonio held her at arm's length and boomed, "You always say that, Mama."

The terrible truth dawned. Cassie gaped at the two. Of course! Mother and son! They even possessed the same striking features, the same coloring, the same bright buoyancy of spirit.

Good heavens, thought Cassie. What awful things did I say to Juliana about Antonio? That he was reclusive, a snob...oh, why didn't I keep my big mouth shut!

Juliana tucked her slim arm in Antonio's and smiled in gentle amusement at Cassie. "Antonio, Miss Rowlands was very impressed with your music.

So impressed that she has invited us to see her perform tomorrow night at her church. Are we free?''

Antonio flashed a quizzical smile. ''Are you a singer also, Miss Rowlands?''

''No, I—I'm a pianist.''

He studied her with an intensity that left her feeling weak inside. ''You look familiar, Miss Rowlands. Have I seen you perform?''

She struggled to find her voice. ''No. I teach a couple of piano classes here at the university. We've passed each other in the fine arts building or on campus.''

''Ah, yes, that's it. I knew I had seen you before. I would never forget such a lovely face.''

Cassie's cheeks grew warm with a dizzying mixture of pleasure and embarrassment. ''You're very kind, Mr. Pagliarulo.''

''Call me Antonio, please. After all, we are colleagues.''

''Then please call me Cassandra. Or Cassie.''

''I prefer Cassandra. It has the lilting ring of music. Now tell me about your performance tomorrow evening.''

Cassie groped for words. What was there about Antonio Pagliarulo that left her feeling so rattled and unsure of herself? ''It's—it's not a big production really,'' she stammered. ''Just a little church cantata at—at Cornerstone Christian in La Jolla. I happened to invite your mother, but I didn't realize...I mean, I'm sure a musician of your stature must have other obligations.''

Antonio clasped her hand reassuringly. ''Not at

all, Cassandra. Mother and I reserve our Sundays for worship. We would be pleased to come hear you perform at your church tomorrow night. It would be a treat to be in the audience for a change instead of onstage.''

''Wonderful,'' said Cassie, her smile so tight she feared her teeth might break. What had she gotten herself into? She would be a basket case performing before this man. Had she somehow taken leave of her senses? Until this evening Antonio Pagliarulo had been a stranger to her; now suddenly his opinion of her mattered more than anything she could imagine.

Chapter Four

Andrew Rowlands was sitting in his squeaky rocker by the bay window in his bedroom, listening to the clock strike midnight and wondering why his oldest daughter hadn't come home yet. Usually this was his favorite place for studying the Bible and thinking and praying. And, at times like this, worrying. How could he sleep well until he knew all of his daughters were safely in for the night?

Still, he chided himself for fretting. Cassie had gone to a concert with a man who seemed harmless enough—a mild-mannered fellow who looked like a bookish and absentminded professor. He was surely not Cassie's type, but then, who on earth was Cassie's type? Except for that one unfortunate incident years ago, she had never been serious about any man. And to make matters even more frustrating for Andrew, she didn't even appear to be looking for a suitable young man. At this rate she would surely end up an old maid.

All right, they didn't call them that anymore. *Old maids.* These days there was no stigma attached to being unattached. Unmarried. Lots of young women preferred the single life.

But that's not what Andrew wanted for his daughters. He wouldn't be around forever to look after his girls, and after he was gone, who would be there for them? Sure, they had one another, but they each needed a strong, capable, trustworthy man to be there when the road got tough.

"Mandy, what are we going to do about our girls?" Andrew said aloud in a soft, husky voice. He gazed out at the full moon hanging in the dark heavens like a beacon light. That pale white globe was always comforting, reassuring. That familiar moon had remained steady and bright in the night sky, sometimes full and brimming, sometimes little more than a fingernail, but so often there through his long nights of grieving.

It was as if God had personally given Andrew the moon and stars for his own private comfort. They were reminders that God Himself was there, never changing, always ready to console. Andrew couldn't have made it these past five years without God's sweet solace.

"Lord, I'm concerned about my girls," he said, rubbing his hands thoughtfully. "I want them to have husbands and families of their own, but they still seem perfectly content to stay here at home with me. As much as I enjoy having them around, I think it's high time they stop fussing over me and establish their own lives and homes. What do you think, Lord?

I'm right, aren't I?'' He shook his head ponderously. ''But I can't tell them to move out. It would break their hearts to think I don't need them anymore. And to be honest, Lord, I do need them.''

Andrew gazed off into the shadows of his room for a moment. He had prayed this prayer often in recent days, but he still didn't have an answer to his dilemma.

In the old days his dear Mandy always knew what to do. She was the perfect mother with just the right balance of love and discipline. He still remembered how she would check on the girls each night. Like a fragile wraith in her long white cotton nightgown, her red hair twining around her shoulders, she would flit from room to room, peeking in the door to be sure her daughters were slumbering peacefully. Andrew hadn't realized what an arduous task and yet what a privilege mothering was until he was forced to be both mother and father.

''Mandy, I'm doing the best I can for our daughters, but I sure miss you, sweetheart.'' He sat forward and raked his fingers through his thick russet hair. ''And I know the girls have suffered deeply from the loss of their mother. Cassie has thrown herself into her music career. Practices hours every day. She's beautiful, talented and ambitious, but sometimes I think she puts all of her emotions into the piano, so she won't feel the pain of losing you...plus that no-good scoundrel who broke her heart the year after you died. Sure, Cassie loves her music, but that won't replace the love of a good man someday.''

Andrew put his head in his hands. ''And our dar-

ling Bree is much too serious about her counseling
work. She's always helping others and bringing
home every poor, needy soul who needs a place to
stay, but she refuses to allow herself a serious romantic relationship. And Frannie, our baby, has taken
over the household and does the cooking and
watches over me like a little mother hen. But she
should be pampering a husband, not me.''

Andrew stared up again at the star-studded sky,
moisture gathering in his eyes. "You would know
what to do, Mandy. You would know how to encourage and guide our daughters in matters of the
heart. You would know how to set them free and
shoo them out of the nest so they could create their
own homes and families. Me, I'm awkward at these
things. I don't know the right words. You know me
better than anyone, Mandy. You polished a lot of
rough edges, but I'm still a bull in the china shop.
All thumbs. Two left feet. I wish I had your sensi-
tivity, your knack for reading our daughters' moods
and knowing what they needed even before they
asked. I've asked God to help me, but—''

A noise came from downstairs. Andrew paused,
listening. Yes, it was the front door. Cassie was
home. He got up and walked out to the landing and
looked down. Cassie was standing in the foyer, stepping out of her high heels, the overhead lamplight
turning her tousled mane of hair to spun gold.

He tied the sash of his robe and padded downstairs
in his leather slippers. Cassie looked up and smiled
as he approached.

"Hi, Daddy. What are you doing up at this hour?''

"Waiting for you," he confessed.

"Daddy, I'm twenty-six years old. You don't have to wait up for me anymore."

He grinned sheepishly. "I know. Can't help myself."

Picking up her shoes, Cassie walked in her stockinged feet to the living room and sank down on the overstuffed sofa.

"Tired?" he asked, following a step behind.

She nodded.

"Have fun?"

Another nod, and the hint of a playful smile.

"So Gilbert what's-his-name wasn't so bad after all?"

Cassie chuckled. "Oh, he was just what I expected, but nice enough in a cerebral sort of way. If you happen to like walking textbooks."

Andrew sat down in the recliner across from his daughter. "So if your date was nothing to write home about, why the mysterious little smile?"

Cassie's face flushed crimson. "Oh, Daddy, you're not supposed to notice that smile."

"Really? Maybe I'm getting better at this parenting thing than I thought. So tell me, or my imagination will run wild, and we don't want that, do we?"

"Okay, but it's nothing really." Cassie pulled the pins from her French twist and gracefully swept her fingertips through her cascading curls. "I met a couple of interesting people tonight, that's all."

"Of the masculine persuasion, I trust?"

"A man and a woman."

"Married?"

"Mother and son. What is this, Daddy, twenty questions?"

"Just want to know what has put that new light in your eyes."

She lowered her long lashes. "Daddy, really, there's nothing to it. I just met the man who performed tonight. A very talented tenor."

"Single?"

"I assume so. I got the impression he lives at home with his mother."

Andrew's thick brows arched. "His mother? Not a mama's boy, I hope."

"Oh, Daddy, you wouldn't say that if you saw him." Cassie rushed on before her father could interrupt again. "I met his mother quite by accident. At the reception. We got to talking and, Daddy, she's an absolutely fascinating woman..."

Andrew sat back in his chair and tented his fingers. "Okay, I've got it, muffin. She's my age and single and coming to dinner tomorrow night. Am I right so far?"

"Not coming to dinner, Daddy. There's the cantata. But I did suggest getting a bite to eat afterward."

"And this time we'll make it a threesome instead of a double date. The tenor's mother and Lydia Diddlehopper..." he said dryly.

"Dibbles."

"And Emma Sawhorse, of course."

"Sorenson! Really, Daddy, you think you're so clever."

Andrew sat forward and eyed his daughter intently. "I'm just trying to make a point, Cass. No matchmaking. You hear me?"

She examined one long polished fingernail. "Of course, I hear you, Daddy. I'm not matchmaking. You're just being your usual paranoid self. Besides, what makes you think I'm trying to pair you up with Antonio's mother?"

"Who's Antonio?"

"The tenor. Antonio Pagliarulo."

Andrew grinned. "I like the way you say his name."

Cassie pointed one red lacquered fingernail at her father. "Now who's matchmaking?"

Andrew raised his hands in a gesture of conciliation. "Just making a small observation!"

"All Italian names roll off the tongue like that. It's one of the romance languages, after all."

"Romance? Is there the possibility we're speaking of more than languages here?"

Cassie crossed her arms resolutely. "Not a chance, Daddy. Mr. Pagliarulo is a snob, a recluse, a loner. Everyone says so."

"And that was your impression of him?"

Cassie chose her words carefully. "We met only for a few moments. He seemed nice enough."

"Well, unless you plan to see him again, I suppose you'll never know what he's really like."

"Oh, I'm going to see him again," Cassie said quickly.

Andrew shook his head, puzzled. "But you said—"

"I didn't invite Antonio and his mother over for dinner, but I did invite them to the cantata. They agreed to come."

Andrew grinned knowingly. "I see. And you're hoping I'll hit it off with...with..."

"Juliana."

"Juliana?"

"Juliana Pagliarulo. She's beautiful, Daddy. And so full of life and spirit. I know you'll like her."

Andrew got up and crossed over to the sofa and planted a kiss on the top of his daughter's head. "Maybe we'd better get some sleep, baby. It sounds like tomorrow will be quite a day."

Cassie caught her father's hand. "Oh, and Daddy, one more thing."

He paused. "I hate to ask."

In a small voice Cassie said, "I invited Antonio and Juliana to join us for dinner after the program. Maybe that little Italian restaurant near the church?"

Andrew sighed. "All right, Cass. On one condition."

"Of course. What is it, Daddy?"

"No matchmaking!"

Just a hint of mischief played in Cassie's smile. "I'll promise if you promise."

"Promise," said Andrew. But as he climbed the stairs to his room, he was already imagining his beloved daughter looking exquisite in a white bridal gown of satin and lace. She would be standing at the altar on the arm of a handsome Italian tenor, as Andrew, the proud papa, pronounced them husband and wife.

Yes, indeed, mused Andrew, tomorrow promised to be a fascinating day!

But on Sunday afternoon Andrew began to suspect that perhaps Cassie shouldn't have invited her two guests, for never had he seen his daughter so agitated before a performance. Three times she checked to make sure the sound system was operating properly. At rehearsal she fretted over how the choir sounded, and whether the program was too long, and whether the church auditorium was too warm.

Finally, a half hour before the cantata, Andrew stopped his daughter backstage and gripped both her hands in his. "Why are you so nervous, Cass? Where is this coming from?"

She shook her head miserably. "I don't know, Daddy. I just can't seem to get it together tonight."

"Maybe because you're trying to make this something it's not. You're performing in a nice little church cantata, honey, not Carnegie Hall. I'm sure your Italian tenor will understand that."

"He's not my Italian tenor," she snapped.

Andrew smiled tolerantly. "All right. The point is you're not in competition with him."

"I don't even think I can play." She held up trembling hands. "Look at me, Daddy."

"I'm looking, sweetheart. You're beautiful and talented and you're going to be fine. Just relax and go out there and enjoy yourself."

"Relax? How can I, with Antonio Pagliarulo in the audience?"

"Honey, you're forgetting something. You're not

playing just for Antonio. You're performing for the Lord.''

A tear glistened in the corner of Cassie's clear blue eyes. "I know, Daddy. It's just…why does everything always have to be a competition with me? Why do I feel I always have to be the best?"

"Maybe because you're my oldest daughter and you feel you have to be an example for everyone else. But you don't, sweetheart. Just be yourself."

Cassie touched his cheek. "You're so wise. I love you, Daddy."

Andrew slipped his arm around her shoulders and drew her close. "Cass, let's ask God to give us a great evening, okay? Then you go out there and play your heart out."

They prayed briefly, then exchanged a quick hug. "I wonder if they're here yet?" She peered out through the curtain at the audience, then looked back at her father. "I guess it doesn't matter. I'll just do my best and leave the rest with the Lord."

"That's the spirit, honey. And I'll be applauding you all the way."

To Andrew's relief the cantata went without a hitch. The choir sang with spirit and vitality, and Cassie's piano solos were the best he'd ever heard. If anything, her performance exhibited a new gusto and passion. He felt a thrill of pride as he watched her deft fingers scaling the keys, filling the auditorium with the triumphant strains of a Mozart concerto. She accompanied the choir in several selections she had adapted from Beethoven's Choral and

Pastoral symphonies, then concluded the program with a moving Beethoven sonata.

As the audience broke into resounding applause, Andrew clapped the loudest, his eyes misting as he reflected silently, Oh, my dear Mandy, if only you could have seen our daughter performing this evening. You would be so proud, so very proud!

After the cantata, Andrew greeted his parishioners in the vestibule, nodding with fatherly pride as they complimented the performance. "Wonderful program...such talent...like a choir of angels...such glorious music gives us a little taste of heaven."

"Indeed it does...yes, amen," Andrew was saying when he spotted Cassie coming toward him with a handsome man on one arm and a very attractive woman on the other.

Cassie was beaming. "Daddy, this is Antonio Pagliarulo and his mother, Juliana Pagliarulo. Antonio and Juliana, this is my father, Reverend Andrew Rowlands."

Andrew couldn't take his eyes off Juliana. She was everything Cassie had described...and so much more. Exotic. Poised. Glamorous. Regal. Stunning. Her dark eyes flashed with vibrance and warmth, her flawless, bronze skin glowed, her black-velvet tresses shone. She offered her hand and he clasped it in both of his. "It's a pleasure to meet you, Mrs. Paglia—"

"Juliana, please."

"Of course. Juliana." The name seemed to dance on his lips.

"The pleasure is ours, Reverend. My son and I enjoyed the program very much."

"Call me Andrew. *Reverend* sounds so...stodgy."

"Andrew. A fine name." Juliana's smile enveloped him in its warmth. "And your daughter...she is so talented."

Andrew realized suddenly, to his embarrassment, that he had neglected Antonio, who stood waiting to shake his hand. Andrew turned and gripped the young man's hand perhaps a bit too hard. "Mr. Pagliarulo, my daughter tells me you are a very gifted man yourself."

He returned the firm handshake. "Thank you, sir. Your daughter is very generous in her praise. And, may I say, she is a marvelous pianist."

Andrew chuckled heartily. "Sounds like we have a mutual admiration society going on here, if you ask me."

Cassie clasped her father's arm. "Daddy, I told Antonio we'll be having dinner at the Palazzo Ristorante on La Jolla Boulevard."

"Yes, I think you'll like it. The food's great," Andrew told Antonio. "It's about six blocks from here. Would you like to ride over with us?"

"That won't be necessary," said Antonio. "I have my car."

"You could follow us," suggested Cassie.

"No, I know the restaurant. It's one of my favorites."

Cassie smiled. "I thought it might be."

Andrew turned confidentially to his daughter. "Are your sisters joining us?"

"No, they both said they have previous commitments."

"I'll bet," he said under his breath. He looked back at Antonio and Juliana. "Are we ready to go?"

During the brief drive to the restaurant, Andrew noticed a smile playing on his daughter's lips. He hated succumbing to his suspicious nature, but he couldn't help wondering if Cassie was anticipating a delightful evening with the handsome Antonio Pagliarulo, or was she conniving ways of pairing off her father with the lovely Juliana? Guess we'll just have to wait and see who wins at this matchmaking game, he mused silently.

Palazzo was a quaint, dimly lit café with lots of greenery surrounding cozy tables with red-checkered tablecloths. A jug with a flickering candle and a slim vase with a single red rose graced each table. The walls boasted a series of bright, impressionistic paintings of Venice and Naples. Tantalizing aromas of garlic, olive oil and oregano assailed Andrew's senses as the hostess led them to a table in a private corner. His mouth watered as he caught glimpses of plates piled high with steamy baked manicotti and fettuccini smothered in creamy alfredo sauce. To his surprise he was hungrier than he had felt in days.

"What's good tonight?" he asked the waitress, a young woman with a pretty face and black hair piled on her head in an odd little twist.

"The linguini alla portafino is good if you like shrimp and clams in a rich cream sauce," she said in a high, singsong voice as she placed a basket of garlic bread on the table. "And everyone likes the veal parmigiana. But my favorite is the tortellini calabrese."

"And what is that exactly?" Cassie asked, looking up from her menu.

"Meat tortellini and sausage in marinara sauce topped with mozzarella cheese. It's awesome."

Cassie nodded. "Okay, I'll take your word for it."

Juliana handed the waitress her menu. "I'll just have an antipasto salad, please."

"I'll have the linguini alla portafino," said Antonio.

"I'll try the tortellini," Andrew said. "And bring us an appetizer, okay? Some of those sauteed mushrooms and fried calamari. Might as well do this thing up right." He looked over at Cassie and grinned. "Looks like I should have brought our bibs for a feast like this, right, muffin?"

Cassie's face reddened. "Oh, Daddy, really!"

"Bibs?" echoed Juliana.

Andrew grinned. "We have these big, wonderful bibs we use at home on spaghetti nights. I'm as klutzy as they come, but those bibs work wonders."

"Daddy, Juliana doesn't want to hear about our bibs," Cassie admonished.

"Oh, but I do. What a clever idea."

Andrew chuckled. "You'll have to come over for spaghetti sometime and try them out." The words were out before he realized what he had said.

Juliana met his gaze for a long moment, her dark eyes flashing with merriment. "I'd love to, Andrew," she said softly, her beguiling Mona Lisa smile curling the corners of her lips. Andrew couldn't pull his eyes away from that smile, couldn't stop the sudden roller-coaster tickle in his stomach. Maybe he was coming down with something, the way his heart was racing and his face was feeling flushed. Had to be a fever coming on. The flu maybe. You might know. He'd probably be sick in bed on his day off tomorrow.

Or maybe it wasn't the flu at all. Maybe he was having an allergic reaction to...to Juliana!

He was more than a little relieved when the waitress brought their food. As he bit into a crusty slice of garlic bread, he resolved that he would have to watch his step around this woman. She had a way of making him feel like a bumbling, tongue-tied teenager again. Why did she have to look at him that way, as if she could see through to his heart and read his very thoughts?

"Andrew," she said in her light, lyrical voice. "Andrew?"

He cleared his throat and stared at her. "Yes?"

"You were staring. I thought you were about to say something."

His composure shattered, he groped for a suitable answer. "Yes, you're absolutely right, Juliana. I was about to say—"

"You were going to ask her about her life, weren't you, Daddy?" prompted Cassie.

"Her life? Yes, of course."

"Ask her about her music," Antonio said. "Mama is quite an accomplished performer in her own right."

Andrew gave Juliana an appraising glance. "Is that so? Do you sing?"

Juliana gazed down at her plate. "From time to time."

Antonio reached over and squeezed his mother's hand. "Mama is too modest. She has performed in concerts around the world."

"When I was young," Juliana protested. "Rarely do I sing anymore."

"Why not?" prodded Andrew. "Cassie and I would love to hear you sing sometime."

"And I would love to hear you deliver a sermon, Andrew."

"Oh, he's good at delivering sermons," Cassie teased.

Juliana laughed lightly. "I mean, from the pulpit. I imagine you are a very eloquent man."

"Eloquent? I doubt that. But I do try to help folks catch a glimpse of what God has for them in His Word."

"Then I will come hear you some Sunday morning. Unless there's a better time."

"Actually, our church is joining with several others for a city-wide crusade in November. I'll be preaching every evening during the week... presenting some of my favorite messages."

"Wonderful. Perhaps Antonio and I will come hear you."

An idea struck. "You could do better than that. You could come sing for us."

"Me? Sing for you?" A radiant glow suffused Juliana's face. The blush of modesty had never looked so lovely. "Oh, Andrew! I couldn't! I do not sing for large crowds anymore."

He retreated, feeling a discomfiting warmth around his collar. "I'm sorry. I didn't mean to put you on the spot or embarrass you. Sometimes I blurt things out without thinking."

Juliana placed her slim hand over his. "Do not apologize. I am flattered. And touched by your offer. But I am not the one you should be asking. Antonio is the one who should sing for your crusade."

Andrew broke into a grin. "Maybe you're right, Juliana." He gazed across the table at Antonio. "How about it? Would you consider singing for our city-wide crusade?"

Antonio looked over at Cassie, as if to gauge her reaction.

Cassie beamed. "Oh, Antonio, please! We would be honored to have you sing at the crusade!"

"I'll check my calendar, and let you know. But I think we can work something out."

Andrew nodded, pleased. "And I'll submit your name to the committee. It's just a formality. I'm sure they'll approve."

Antonio cast another searching glance at Cassie and said with a hint of merriment, "I'll sing, Cassandra, on one condition."

"What's that?" she asked with a note of caution.

"That you accompany me on the piano."

Cassie sank back in her seat. "Oh, I couldn't."

Antonio squeezed her hand. "Of course you can. We will do a marvelous duet together. Everyone will be enchanted."

Andrew's grin deepened. He broke into silent applause. "Wonderful! Splendid! I'll arrange every-

thing. The two of you will make beautiful music together!"

"Daddy!" cried Cassie in the scolding, horrified
tone she reserved for her father's worst blunders.

"It's just a figure of speech, muffin," he said in
his most conciliatory voice. But privately, seeing the
two of them together—his darling daughter and her
handsome tenor—he had a feeling this was the beginning of something more than a musical duet. God
willing, it was the blossoming of a rare and beautiful
relationship.

Chapter Five

On a balmy Friday evening two weeks after the cantata Cassie pulled into the parking lot at her father's church. She was to meet Antonio at seven to rehearse their numbers for the upcoming city-wide crusade, but she was tempted to turn around and drive home. It was crazy. Her stomach was in knots and her emotions on edge, jumbled. She was as nervous as a cat on a high tension wire. She yearned to see Antonio again and yet dreaded facing him, fearful he might expect more of her than she could deliver.

That was it, of course. How could she play the piano for Antonio when she felt so jittery she wasn't even sure her fingers would strike the correct keys? How had she allowed her father to talk her into accompanying Antonio at the crusade?

Actually, it was Antonio who had insisted she accompany him. Was he doing it to torture her, to make her look bad, to show her up as a mediocre musician? Surely not, and yet that's exactly how she felt. He could have chosen the most accomplished pianist in Southern California...but he had asked Cassie. Why hadn't she just said no?

It still wasn't too late to back out. She could simply make some excuse and leave. Surely it wouldn't be hard for Antonio to find another pianist....

But the moment Cassie entered the sanctuary and saw Antonio standing beside the grand piano as he sorted through some sheet music, her heart did a double flip, and she knew she was glad she had come. No matter how terrified she felt at the prospect of accompanying him at the crusade, it was worth the discomfort just to be in his presence again. Surely he was the most handsome man she had ever seen, with that distinctive Roman nose and square jaw and high forehead. And when he looked up at her and smiled, those dark, brooding eyes flecked with gold and amber held her spellbound. Did he like what he saw? She was wearing a pale-blue pantsuit and stacked heels. Was she overdressed? Underdressed? How did one dress for an occasion like this? It was more of a nonoccasion, not a date certainly. Not a date. Then why did she care so much how she looked and what he thought of her?

"Hello, Cassandra." His gentle voice felt almost like an embrace.

Cassie was breathless. "Hello, Antonio. I hope I'm not late."

His eyes crinkled, flashing warmth and amusement. "Not at all. I must have been early." As she approached he stepped forward and gave her a brief embrace, the kind one gives a casual friend. But his closeness—his smooth cheek against hers, the lime fragrance of his aftershave—was enough to send Cassie's senses reeling.

In his easy, graceful stride he walked back over to the piano and arranged the sheet music on the stand. "I guess we should get started. Are you ready?"

She sat down on the piano bench and smiled up at him. Could he hear her pounding heart? Sense her nervousness? "I'm as ready as I'll ever be."

For all of her anxieties and trepidation, the evening went like clockwork. Like magic. As Antonio sang and she played, something extraordinary happened. They performed as one, in perfect synchronicity, as if they had spent their entire lives performing together. Each seemed to know instinctively what the other was about to do; even their musical interpretations matched.

Cassie found herself feeling pleased, exultant, even euphoric. She sensed a new excitement and passion in her playing, a fresh burst of confidence. It was as if Antonio had unwittingly freed some deep creative impulse within her.

After their rehearsal, as Antonio walked Cassie to her car, he said with a hint of levity, "My dear lady, was it my imagination, or did we sound sensational together?"

She hesitated, struggling for words. "You...you sounded superb, I know that much."

"But there was something magical, electric going on here tonight," he persisted. "Didn't you feel it?

It's not always that way when I sing. Admit it, Cassandra. We were soaring." He touched her arm gently. "Please, don't tell me it was all one-sided. Am I wrong?"

"No, I felt it too. It was...extraordinary."

He chuckled. "Now if we just sound as good to the rest of the world, we'll be all set."

He opened her door for her, then clasped her arm before she stepped inside. "Cassandra, wait. I have an idea. I'm too jazzed to just go home and call it a night. Would you like to go somewhere? Get something to eat?"

She was about to say she wasn't hungry, but quickly canceled the remark and said instead, "Yes. I'd like that."

"More Italian cuisine?"

"No, it's too late for a big fancy meal. How about the little coffee shop around the corner? They've got great burgers."

"Burgers it is. Why don't you leave your car here and ride with me?"

She looked up and caught his infectious smile. "Okay, Antonio. Lead the way."

He escorted her across the parking lot to a large luxury sedan, a deep burgundy color with a black leather interior. He opened her door and she slipped inside. "A beautiful car."

"Not as beautiful as its passenger." He lingered a moment, his eyes fastened on her, then went around to his side, got in, and they were off.

As he drove she cast several surreptitious glances at his finely chiseled profile. He was a gorgeous man, no doubt about it! Even in sport shirt and slacks he looked debonair. And yet he seemed completely unaware of his stunning good looks.

In the coffee shop, as they ordered burgers and fries, she realized he looked too cosmopolitan for a greasy spoon like this. She fidgeted with her water glass, the napkin, the silverware, silently chastising herself for not suggesting a more sophisticated restaurant.

But once their burgers were served, Antonio seemed quite at home and ate with genuine relish, as if burgers were his favorite repast. Halfway through the meal he leaned over and touched her lips with his fingertips. She thought for an instant he was going to kiss her, but instead of whispering sweet endearments, he simply said, "Ketchup."

Embarrassment sent a flush of warmth to her face. "I'm sorry. I'm such a klutz."

"Don't be sorry. It's a lovely face with or without that tiny dollop of ketchup."

"I'm like my dad. I need one of his spaghetti bibs."

"And you promised to show me those one of these days."

"I will. Whenever you and your mother come over for one of our spaghetti dinners."

He traced the ring of his water glass. "We should make it soon. I think my mother is quite taken with your father."

Cassie's eyes widened. "You think so?"

"I know so. She's mentioned his name a number

of times since the four of us went to dinner together."

Cassie smiled. "I think my father is quite infatuated with your mother, as well. She's a beautiful woman."

"Yes, she's quite remarkable, especially considering that she's had to go it alone for so many years."

"How long has it been, if you don't mind my asking? How long since your father died?"

"A long time. I was just a boy when he died."

"Was it an illness?"

"No." A long pause. "An accident."

"I'm sorry. It must have been very painful for you, losing your father at such a young age."

"It was. But then you lost your mother. You know how hard it is."

She lowered her gaze. "Yes, I do. But I was grown. Almost twenty-one."

Antonio drummed his fingers on the polished tabletop. "I was ten. I stopped being a child that day."

"I don't mean to pry...but was it a car accident?"

He looked sharply at her, his jaw tightening. "How did you know?"

She retreated. "I didn't. I guessed. But maybe you'd rather not talk about it."

"It's in the past. There's nothing to say." He looked off in the distance for a moment; then as he gazed back at her, his expression softened. "I'd rather talk about the little spark I noticed between your father and my mother."

Cassie laughed lightly. "My father has often accused my sisters and me of playing the matchmaker. We've always denied it, but in this case I may have to plead guilty.''

A curious smile flickered on Antonio's lips. ''Are you saying you're trying to get our parents together—my mother, your father?''

Cassie's cheeks grew warm. ''I'm not trying to marry them off exactly, but I would like to see my father have some female companionship.''

''I would think there are dozens of eligible ladies in his church who might desire his affections.''

''There are, but he's never paid much attention to them. It's as if, since Mom died, he's turned off that part of his life. I hate to say it, but in some ways it's like he died with my mother. I mean, sometimes I even hear him talking to her, as if she were there in the room with him. I don't think that's healthy, do you?''

Antonio shrugged. ''All I know is that my mother is very much like your father—not in personality, of course. In that sense they're as different as night and day. But in the way she has dealt with her grief. She lives a very full, productive life, but she avoids even the hint of a relationship with a man. If a man tries to get close to her, she immediately cuts off the relationship.''

''I know what you mean,'' Cassie said. ''My father hides behind his three daughters. We're always his excuse...the reason he can't go here or there or do this or that. He's made us his life. None of us has dared leave home. We're afraid Dad will fall apart if the family breaks up. Not fall apart exactly, but deteriorate. Become a hermit, a recluse. We all try hard to still be his little girls, but we can't go on like this forever."

"You're right," Antonio agreed as he polished off the last morsel of his burger. "You need to be free to have a life of your own. You and your sisters."

"Yes, I do. We do!" Cassie smoothed out her straw wrapper, making it very neat and flat. "But it's not like I have some man waiting in the wings. Not like I want to run off and get married. It's nothing like that."

"Oh, of course not. I wasn't implying…"

"I mean, there could be someone…there have been men I've dated, some very nice men…"

"I'm sure. Very suitable, no doubt."

"Yes, suitable. But nothing serious." Except for one. Drake Cameron. But she refused to think of him now. She inhaled deeply and declared, "I have no intention of getting serious with anyone until I've established my career."

Antonio sat forward, his elbows on the table, his gaze solemn and direct. "A wise decision, Cassandra. I've made the same choice for myself. I have more than enough responsibilities already to occupy my time. And I have many goals. I will not always be a university professor, teaching others how to sing. I intend to work hard to carve out a niche for myself in the world of classical music. And I will not let any woman complicate my life until I am well established. That, of course, may take years. Perhaps even then I will prefer the single life."

Cassie nodded. "I admire your drive and determination."

"And I respect your pluck and honesty. Very refreshing."

Cassie sipped her iced tea. "I'm glad we've had this little talk, Antonio. It feels good to speak so openly, to be so frank."

"Indeed. To say what's on our minds."

"Absolutely. So often these days men and women play such silly little games...."

He flashed a wry grin. "Yes, they do. Foolish, inane schemes to woo one another. I detest such duplicity."

"Oh, so do I," said Cassie fervently.

Antonio's voice deepened. "Why can't people say exactly what they think and feel and let the chips fall where they may?"

Cassie's pulse quickened with excitement. This was truly a man after her own heart. "I feel that way exactly, Antonio. I have no patience with all the subterfuge and artifice involved in courtship today. A man brings a woman flowers and tells her how special she is and then treats her as if she's just another dish, his...his flavor of the week."

Antonio's brows arched in surprise; his umber-brown eyes glinted with concern. "Has that happened often, Cassandra?"

"To me?" She touched her throat, flustered. Had she said too much? "Oh, no, not often, but enough to make me skeptical when I hear a fancy line. You know. 'Where have you been all my life?' That sort of thing. That's why I'm so turned off to dating. It's always the same old thing. Lots of sweet talk, hearts and flowers, then, 'Your place or mine?' "

A mixture of tenderness and bemusement flickered in Antonio's eyes. "You are jaded, aren't you? Someone must have hurt you deeply."

Cassie gazed down at her half-eaten burger. A pang of memory pierced her for a moment. Drake Cameron. Why couldn't she forget? Why couldn't she put him out of her mind once and for all? She pushed the memory away, ignoring the pain. "Someone did hurt me once, but it's not something I want to remember."

"And now I'm prying, is that it?"

She studied Antonio for a moment. He had a good face, handsome, of course, but there was so much more in his expression. Integrity, sincerity, compassion. She smiled. "Honesty is good, but some things are better left unsaid. You would rather not talk about your father's death. I'd rather not talk about the men in my life." She chuckled. "Not that there have been that many, believe me."

"I do. And I will respect your wishes." He reached across the table and touched her hand. "If we're going to be friends, it's good to know where we both stand."

She smiled. "I agree. I like that. Being friends. Without complications or expectations."

"Actually, we will be more than friends," Antonio said.

"More than friends?"

He laughed. "Didn't we agree to be colleagues in a friendly little conspiracy...?"

"Oh, you mean our parents. Of course!"

"To help them discover a happier, more fulfilling life?"

"To encourage their friendship at least," Cassie agreed. She raised her water glass in a mock salute. "To your mother and my father...and whatever the future may bring."

Even as she and Antonio toasted their harmless matchmaking scheme, she had an unsettling feeling in the pit of her stomach. What was it? What was her heart trying to tell her? She had no words for it, but she sensed she was opening the door to a barrage of emotional complications she had never bargained for. And now, as Antonio clasped her hand across the table, she knew it was too late to turn back.

Chapter Six

Andrew was in the best of moods, pleased with himself, elated. Everything was going just as he had planned. Antonio and Juliana were coming over tonight for dinner, and what a dinner it would be! Frannie was fixing her specialty, spaghetti, but she and Bree had already agreed to bow out and leave the two "couples" alone this evening.

Andrew had a feeling Cassie had arranged this "double date" to pair him off with Juliana, but that was okay. He would play along. What Cassie didn't know was that he was orchestrating this evening to give her and Antonio a chance to discover each other in a relaxed, homey setting.

Maybe he was wrong to take matters into his own hands like this, but if he sat around and waited for Cassie to find a suitable beau, he would be a doddering old man and his daughter would be past the age of giving him grandchildren. All he could do was hope Cassie wouldn't resent his intrusion into her love life and that God would forgive him for taking drastic measures to nudge his oldest daughter down the road to matrimony.

It seemed that God was smiling down on all of them. Cassie and Antonio had seen one another at least twice a week this past month as they rehearsed their musical numbers for the crusade. They usually went out to dinner together after rehearsal. And Cassie always came in with that dazed, dreamy look in her eyes and a mysterious little smile on her lips. That had to mean something.

Andrew himself had seen the spark between Cassie and Antonio; it was unmistakable. Even across the room he could feel the electricity between them, the chemistry. Antonio was the man for Cassie, Andrew was sure of it. If it didn't sound a tad presumptuous, he would say God Himself had brought Antonio and Cassie together. Surely in His vast omniscience, God knew how right they were for each other. But no, Andrew didn't dare presume on God's beneficence. He couldn't pretend to know the mind of the Lord. But he could do all within his power to nurture that magic spark between Antonio and his daughter, and then the rest was in the hands of the Almighty.

Andrew took a final glance in his dresser mirror, splashed some cool, biting aftershave on his face, flicked the crisp collar of his sport shirt, and strode on out of his room and down the stairs to the kitchen.

Frannie was just draining the pasta in the colander. She looked around at him, her long hair mussed, fly-away, and her young face glowing with warmth from the stove.

"Smells good in here," Andrew said, dipping a spoon into the spaghetti sauce bubbling on the back burner. "Maybe you and Bree should stay, after all the work you've put in."

"No, Daddy, Bree's seeing a client and I have a date on the sunporch with my sculpture. Don't worry, you won't hear a peep from me. I think it's so sweet you're trying to get Tonio and Cassie together. I think you're right. They could be a match made in heaven."

"Just don't tell her I said so," Andrew warned. "You know she would have a fit if she thought I was playing matchmaker."

"Who's playing matchmaker, Daddy?"

Andrew pivoted sharply and gazed at Cassie in the dining room doorway looking stunning in a red linen pantsuit, her blond hair in a sophisticated, upswept twist.

"Did I say matchmaker?" Andrew asked innocently, racking his brain for a suitable explanation. Face it, he was caught!

"Uh, maybe I was talking about you…or me…playing matchmaker with Juliana and Antonio. So tell me, cupcake, is that why you invited the two of them to dinner?"

Cassie breezed over and planted a kiss on his forehead. "That's for me to know and you to find out, Daddy. Just be on your best behavior, okay? And please, don't bring out the bibs!"

He was saved by the bell. The doorbell.

"It's them!" Cassie was already heading for the door, but she paused to call back, "And, Daddy, none of your lame jokes tonight, please!"

"Lame?" he echoed, feigning indignance as he followed her to the door. "How do I know if they're lame until I've told them?"

As Cassie opened the door, Andrew ran his hand over his hair, drew in a deep breath and straightened his shoulders. Why on earth did he suddenly feel nervous, fidgety, his palms moist? This was going to be Cassie and Antonio's night, not his and—

"Juliana! Welcome!" Andrew boomed as mother and son stepped inside the marble entry. Juliana looked exquisite in a gold, form-fitting dress that accented her bronze skin, red lips and those flowing black tresses. Andrew shook hands with Antonio, but his eyes were still on Juliana.

Effortlessly, instinctively she went into his arms for an embrace. In his arms she felt warm and soft and smelled somehow of roses and raspberries. He felt momentarily breathless as she purred, "Andrew, thank you for having us over."

"Our pleasure," he murmured huskily. From the corner of his eye he noticed Antonio embracing Cassie and giving her a peck on the cheek. So far so good. Everything was on track. Now if he could just get over this warm, dizzy, light-headed feeling Juliana kindled in him.

As the foursome made their way through the living room, Juliana gazed around, her dark eyes flashing fire, dazzling. "Your home is lovely. So cozy and warm and charming. Just like you, Andrew! Oh, and it smells heavenly! Is that your daughter's famous spaghetti?''

He grinned. "Yes, indeed. You'll love it. Money-back guarantee.''

Frannie, in her frilly apron, stepped out from the kitchen and greeted their guests. "Hello, Juliana, Antonio. Hope you're hungry!''

"Starved!'' said Juliana. "Your spaghetti smells divine!''

"Frannie, if you're not Italian, you should be,'' said Antonio. "It smells like my grandmother's house when I was a little boy. *Delizioso!*''

"Frannie does most of the cooking around here,'' said Cassie. "The rest of us can't match her culinary skills, right, Dad?''

"We don't even try.''

Frannie smiled. "I just hope it tastes as good as it smells. You can all sit down whenever you like. The salad's ready.''

"And, dear, after dinner I want to see your sculpture,'' said Juliana. "Your father told me how talented you are.''

Frannie brushed back a wisp of burnished hair. "Daddy's a bit prejudiced. But, sure, I'll show you what I'm doing. I'm just finishing Amelia Earhart. If you like, stop in the sunroom and watch me work.''

"I will, I will! I love creative people. How I wish I could paint or sculpt. I can't even draw silly little stick figures.''

Antonio touched Cassie's arm and smiled. "Cassandra, you have a very talented family.''

"Oh, yes, Frannie's a marvel,'' Cassie agreed.

"Not just Frannie. I mean you."

"Frannie's got her stuff all over the house," said Andrew proudly. "Even a bust of me in the family room. Looks a bit like George Washington, if you ask me."

Frannie put her hands on her hips. "Oh, Daddy, it does not!"

Juliana tucked her arm in Andrew's as they headed for the dining room. "George Washington? That I must see."

Before Andrew could warn his guests, Ruggs came bounding into the room and jumped up on Juliana, pawing, yipping eagerly.

Andrew grabbed for the dog. "Down, boy! Come on, get down!"

"Oh, what a darling!" Juliana stooped down and scratched Ruggs's ears and allowed him to lick her hand. "Oh, you are so happy and full of life, big fellow. You must love living here in this warm, wonderful house!"

"You obviously have a way with dogs," Andrew said, pleased. "I've never seen Ruggs take to anyone like this. It's as if he's known you all his life."

"I love dogs, especially big friendly, affectionate dogs like yours." She gave Andrew a sly grin. "I find that dogs take after their masters. Have you noticed that?"

He laughed, warm-faced, his pulse quickening. No doubt, Juliana had a way about her, and not just with dogs. "So are you saying I'm like Ruggs…big, friendly and affectionate?"

Juliana's eyes snapped impishly. "Aren't you?"

He pulled back a chair for her at the dining table. "Yes, I guess you've got me pegged."

Andrew took the chair across from Juliana while Antonio held a chair for Cassie, then sat down across from her. When they were settled, Andrew held out his hands. "Shall we ask the blessing?" He looked over at Frannie in the kitchen doorway. "Come on, sweetheart, join us." As they linked hands he offered a brief prayer, concluding with, "Thank You, Father, for good food and good company. Keep our hearts filled with gratitude and love."

As everyone whispered amen, Frannie stole back to the kitchen and returned with the tossed salad, rolls and spaghetti, then excused herself to go work on her sculpture.

"Dear, after all your hard work, aren't you going to sit down and join us?" asked Juliana.

Frannie paused. "No, this is Daddy's dinner party. I enjoyed cooking, but now I've really got to get back to my sculpture."

Andrew reached out, caught Frannie's hand, and gave her an impromptu hug. "Thanks, pumpkin. You've created another winner. You're fantastic!"

"Thanks, Daddy. You're the best."

"What a darling girl," Juliana said when Frannie had gone.

"She's quite a little sister," Cassie said. "It's as if she's made it her mission in life to take care of Daddy. Bree and I are gone so much, but Frannie is always here, keeping the home fires burning."

"What about your other daughter?" asked Juliana. "Isn't she joining us?"

"No," Andrew replied. "Brianna has an appointment with a client tonight. She works for a family counseling center. But even when she's not at work, she's on the phone or making house calls, trying to help people. She's amazing. Has a heart as wide as Texas."

"Sometimes she even brings needy people home to stay," Cassie told them. "Remember, Daddy? The woman with three kids whose husband was abusing her? The shelters were full, so Bree brought her and the kids here for a week. It started feeling like a child-care center around here. Of course, Ruggs was in his glory with all the attention."

Andrew passed Juliana the salad. "Actually, that's how we got Ruggs. Bree was just a teenager when she found this scruffy stray dog walking with a limp. She brought him home and he's been with us ever since. It's good that we have a big house. There's always room for one more person…or animal."

Juliana smiled. "That means you are a very kind and generous man, like your daughters."

He shrugged. "I try to be. But sometimes, like anyone else, I fall flat on my face. Figuratively speaking."

Juliana shook her head. "That I cannot imagine."

Andrew handed her the pasta and spaghetti sauce. "Wait till you try the meatballs. They're out of this world."

Juliana forked up a mound of pasta and handed the bowl to Antonio, then turned back suddenly to Andrew. "Wait! Something is missing. Where are our bibs? You told us about the bibs your daughter made."

Andrew pushed back his chair. "You're right. We can't forget the bibs!"

"Oh, Daddy, no, not the bibs! Not tonight!"

Ignoring Cassie's protests, Andrew went to the buffet, removed four bibs and went around the table, triumphantly tying one around each neck.

"Oh, these are delightful!" exclaimed Juliana, straightening hers over her gold dress.

Antonio leaned across the table and patted Cassie's hand. "Don't despair, dear girl. I agree with your father. The bibs are charming. And you look lovely in yours. But then, you would look lovely in anything."

Cassie made a little sad face. "Thanks for trying, Antonio, but you're just too much of a gentleman to laugh."

He chuckled. "If I laughed at you, then you could laugh at me. We are all in the same boat, are we not?"

"And a tasty little boat it is," Andrew said. "Forget fretting over your bib, muffin, and help yourself to the spaghetti. It's dynamite!"

Once Cassie resigned herself to wearing the bib, the meal progressed without incident. The conversation was light, leisurely and nearly as delectable as the food.

After dinner Cassie brought out a colorful ice cream confection called spumoni mountain. She served frosty slices of the rainbow dessert on small china plates with fancy cookies and demitasse cups of hot, black coffee.

Andrew's favorite. He was in his glory.

After dinner they lingered at the table, sipping their coffee, sampling another cookie or two.

"I don't know about all of you, but I'm too stuffed to move," Andrew said.

"I might make it into the next room, but that's about it," Antonio added, removing his bib.

Cassie removed hers, too. "I would love to show you the music room, Antonio. Especially the grand piano. It's been in the family for years. Come. It's just down the hall."

He pushed back his chair. "I think I can make it that far." He turned to Juliana. "Mama, do you want to join us?"

Cassie broke in. "Oh, Daddy, why don't you show Juliana the garden? It may not be like springtime with everything blooming, but it's still beautiful. You love gardens, don't you, Juliana?"

"Yes, I do, but I also love music. And lovely old pianos."

Andrew got up and pulled back Juliana's chair and bent close to her ear. "I think they would like to be alone. Or maybe, more accurately, they would like us to be alone."

Juliana stood and removed her bib. "Then the garden it is."

He led her out the back door and across the expansive moonlit yard to a white gazebo nestled among rosebushes and a variety of plants and flowers Andrew couldn't begin to name.

"Watch your step." Taking Juliana's hand, he guided her up the shadowed steps to a wrought-iron bench. They sat down, not close, but close enough that her perfume, that intriguing blend of roses and raspberries, mingled with the earthy fragrance of the garden. "One of the advantages of living in Southern California," he mused, breaking off a red rose and handing it to her. "A few hearty roses still on the bushes in mid-October."

"Thank you, Andrew. It's beautiful," she said, lifting the petals to her nose and inhaling deeply. She gazed around the yard. "I love the smells of the earth and the grass and the night air, with just a hint of the sea. And your garden, Andrew. You must spend a lot of time here making it look so lovely."

Andrew shook his head. "I'd love to take credit for it, but the truth is, this was Mandy's garden. She loved working in it. Since she died I've had a gardener. I don't even know the names of most of these plants and flowers."

Juliana smiled. "At least you are honest." They were both silent for a moment. The whole world seemed to have grown hushed, except for crickets chirruping and the breeze rustling the grass. "How long has it been?" Juliana asked softly.

"You mean, since my wife died?"

"Yes, if you don't mind my asking."

"Five years. Sometimes it seems like days, other times it seems like forever."

"Do you mind talking about her, Andrew? About her death?"

He met Juliana's gaze and marveled at the way the

moonlight glistened on her face, in her hair. He felt too good—his stomach full, the company pleasant—to discuss the event that had nearly shattered his life. "There's not much to tell."

"Of course there is...if the right person is listening. Perhaps I'm not that person."

"I didn't say that."

"I don't want to pry. But I thought perhaps you would like to talk. I imagine it's difficult for a minister to talk about his pain, his needs, when he is the one expected to be strong."

"I suppose you're right."

"And I already know from what I've seen that you would never burden your precious daughters with your sorrows."

Andrew shifted on the bench, moving a bit closer to Juliana. "Right again. You seem to know me pretty well."

She moved toward him, with effortless grace, until she was mere inches away. She looked up at him, her eyes so darkly compelling he couldn't tear his gaze away. "I know how you feel, Andrew, because I have been there myself. For me it has been nearly eighteen years since my husband died, and yet I still relive that terrible night every day of my life."

"Was it an accident?"

"Yes. A car crash." She looked away, her lovely patrician profile etched with silvery light. He could feel her withdrawing from him, erecting a wall.

"And how about you, Juliana?" he prompted. "Maybe you need someone to talk to. Maybe we can listen to each other, comfort each other."

She cleared her throat and massaged her hands, as if mentally preparing herself for a painful ordeal. "It was summer and we were taking a much needed vacation in the Catskill Mountains of New York. We were driving around some steep, hairpin curves, and Marco, my husband, wouldn't slow down. I begged him to, but he wouldn't listen. The car went over the mountain. Marco was thrown from the car and killed instantly, and my...my..." She let her words drift off. She seemed lost in the moment somehow, beyond Andrew's reach, beyond anyone's reach. At last she shook off her reverie and said quietly, "Antonio and I were hurt, but we recovered...in every way except in our hearts."

Andrew reached over and clasped her hand. It was cool and smooth and soft. "I'm so sorry, Juliana. You must have been devastated."

"I was for many years. I was overwhelmed by the burden of it all. But now I have learned to live life again, with joy and hope."

Andrew studied her intently. "I can't help feeling there's more to your story, Juliana. You tell it so matter-of-factly. What have you left out?"

Her hand flinched in his. "Nothing," she said abruptly. "I have told you all there is to say. All that I can tell." She paused and gazed at him. "Now you tell me your story."

He rubbed his palm over her slim fingers. "Okay, but I'm rusty at this. You'll have to be patient with me."

She smiled. "I have the patience of a saint."

He chuckled. "I bet you do."

She shook her head. "All right, I lied. I am not a patient woman. But for you I have all the patience in the world."

"Okay, here goes." He breathed deeply, a restless energy rushing through his veins, making his skin prickle. "It wasn't just one night or a single event that changed everything. It came over us slowly, gradually, insidiously. Mandy was sick a lot. We thought she was just run-down, so she went in for tests. We figured they would show she was anemic, you know? I was sure she just needed more iron or vitamins or something.

"But I could tell by the look on the doctor's face that it was serious. And when he said the *C* word, Mandy and I both broke down and cried."

"Was it treatable?"

"Oh, yeah, for a time. She went the whole miserable route. Chemotherapy. Radiation. Lost her hair, lost her weight and still kept smiling." The nightmarish images flashed in Andrew's mind...Mandy so ill from her treatments she looked like a little ghost, Mandy disappearing from him a little more each day, Mandy so sick all he could do was hold her in his arms and rock her like a hurting child. "Until the very end she was sure she was going to beat it. And because she was sure, so was I."

"It was good to believe, Andrew. She needed your hope, your faith."

He choked back a sob. "And then one day it dawned on me she was dying, and I hadn't even begun to make peace with it, with the cancer, her mortality. It caught me off guard. I realize now I must have gone around with my head in the sand. We kept living as if we had forever, as if we were facing ordinary, routine days. I should have treasured every second we had together. Should have memorized every moment, every word, every look on her face.''

"Don't blame yourself, Andrew.'' Juliana's voice swelled with compassion. "I'm sure Mandy wanted the two of you to live a normal life for as long as you could. I'm sure the normalcy gave her strength and comfort. She didn't want to be treated like an invalid. You did the right thing, Andrew. You made her last days happy and meaningful.''

Andrew felt a rush of tears flood his eyes. He blinked quickly, not wanting Juliana to notice. "How can you know that?'' he challenged. "How can you be so sure I did the right thing?''

She squeezed his hand, her eyes tender, bright. "Because I know you, Andrew. I know in this short time we have been acquainted what kind of man you are. What a good man you are.''

Andrew couldn't pull his gaze from Juliana's eyes, couldn't break the hypnotic spell she had cast on him with her gentle words and tender smile. He felt a sudden impulse to gather her into his arms and kiss her soundly. How he wanted to feel the warmth of her in his arms!

A wave of guilt washed over him. How could he be talking about Mandy and her death one moment and desiring another woman the next? For five long years he had guarded his heart, had kept his devotion and fidelity solely for Mandy. He had refused to look at another woman…as a woman. He had shut down every emotion that might lead him into a romantic entanglement. He had done so well...until now.

Get a grip, he told himself sternly. Don't let a pretty face and some sweet talk turn your head. Think about Mandy, only Mandy! After all, as long as he was true to Mandy, she would remain alive in his heart. It was the least he could do. All he had left of her. To admit he could ever love another woman would be like letting Mandy die all over again. He couldn't tolerate that kind of pain. He had promised to love his wife forever, and that's exactly what he planned to do.

Juliana lifted her hand to his face, her fingertips lightly touching his cheek. "Andrew, are you all right? You look like you've...seen a ghost."

He stood up abruptly and stepped away from Juliana's touch, as if he'd been burned. "I'm fine." His tone was sharp, brittle. "Just felt a sudden chill. You must have felt it, too."

Juliana's voice was subdued. "Yes, Andrew, I felt it."

"So I'd better get you back inside. It's getting late."

"Yes," she said meaningfully. "Maybe it is too late."

Andrew winced inwardly. He could see he had hurt Juliana, disappointed her. But he had no choice. He had to be true to Mandy, to his own resolves. But if he was doing the right thing, why did he feel so incredibly miserable inside?

Chapter Seven

When Cassie went downstairs to breakfast the next morning, her sisters were already at the table sipping their coffee and sharing the newspaper. She sat down and reached for the coffeepot, her head still fuzzy from slumber. She shouldn't have stayed up so late last night.

"Good morning, sunshine," Frannie said, handing her the funnies. "Looks like you had a big night."

Cassie stirred a spoonful of sugar into her cup. "What's that supposed to mean?"

"We're just curious," Bree replied. "How was your evening with Antonio?"

"Fine. Perfectly fine. We had a good time. And Frannie's spaghetti was a hit, as usual."

Bree put her paper aside and sat forward intently. "We're not talking about the food. We want to know if any sparks are flying with your gorgeous Italian tenor."

Cassie sipped her coffee, welcoming its sweet warmth. "Don't be silly. Antonio and I are just friends." She glanced around cautiously. "Where's Dad?"

"In the kitchen," Frannie replied. "Fixing us pancakes."

Cassie stifled a chuckle. "Oh, you know what that means."

"Practical joke time," said Bree. "After all these years you think he'd realize we're on to him."

"We've got to humor him. It's his little way of having fun." Cassie lowered her voice confidentially. "Anyway, what I was saying, Antonio and I are just spending time together to get Dad and his mom together. They're both lonely and could use a little company."

"I think it's a bad idea," Frannie said. "Daddy will never go for it. He still cares too much for Mom."

"Maybe so," said Cassie, "but it's worth a try. It's not like I'm trying to marry him off. I just think he could benefit from a little female companionship once in awhile."

"I'm with Cassie," Bree added. "Juliana is a doll. So fun-loving and personable. If anyone can bring Dad out of himself, it's Juliana."

"She's the exact opposite of Mom," argued Frannie. "Bold and brassy and pushy. Not quiet and refined like Mom. Why would he want to spend time with someone who's nothing like Mom?"

Cassie bristled. "There's nothing that says he has to find someone just like Mom—"

Before Cassie could finish, her father burst in with a platter of steaming pancakes. "Good morning, my darling daughters. Hope you all slept well...and hope you've got a healthy appetite. There are lots more where these came from!" He set the platter on the table and went around and kissed the top of each head, then took his place at the head of the table.

After he asked the blessing—with a distinctive little chuckle in his tone—Bree speared a golden-brown pancake. "Oh, Daddy, these look wonderful, but you shouldn't have!"

Cassie and Frannie exchanged a bemused wink as they helped themselves to the pancakes. This was the same harmless little joke their mother had played on them as children. Since her death, their father had doggedly carried on the tradition despite the fact his girls were too old now to be hoodwinked.

Cassie doused her stack of hotcakes with butter and syrup, then vigorously cut into them. As she suspected they wouldn't cut. She caught her father's mischievous twinkle. "Daddy, you ol' dickens, you're playing one of your April Fool's tricks, and it's not even April."

"If I waited till April, you'd know it was a trick."

Frannie lifted a pancake on her fork. "Look at this! My pancake has a circle of cloth in it. No wonder it won't cut!"

"Mine, too," said Bree, feigning surprise. "Daddy, how could you? Now my mouth is watering for pancakes!"

He pushed back his chair and stood up. "No problem, girls. I've got a whole plate of good ones in the kitchen.'' He was gone and back in a moment with a fresh platter. ''These are the best buttermilk pancakes you'll find anywhere.''

''And no little swatches of material grilled into the bottoms of them?'' challenged Frannie.

He rumpled the top of her head. ''Not a one, baby girl. I'll prove it.'' He sat down and speared several hotcakes and cut into them with his fork. ''See? Light, tender and fluffy. No one makes pancakes like your old man.''

Cassie helped herself and passed the plate on to her sisters. ''You seem in a good mood today, Daddy.''

''Yes, I suppose I am.''

Bree reached for the syrup. ''So, Daddy, does your good mood have anything to do with your date last night?''

''My date? It wasn't exactly a date. Just a nice dinner with friends.''

''You spent quite a bit of time with Juliana out in the garden,'' Cassie said with a sly little smile.

Her father didn't miss a beat. ''I was just giving you and Antonio time to be alone. You seem to enjoy his company.''

''He's very nice,'' Cassie conceded. ''But we're just friends.''

''You spent a lot of time together in the music room,'' Frannie stated. ''Making beautiful music together?''

Cassie laughed. ''Hardly. But we did have fun. We played and sang every old-time camp song and chorus we knew...and a few we didn't know. In fact,

Antonio composed a little song just for me. It's not great poetry or anything, but it was sweet.''

"You're kidding," Bree said. "How romantic!"

"It wasn't romantic. We were just having fun."

Frannie clasped her hands together. "Sing it for us, Cass."

"It's nothing. I don't even know if I remember it."

"Of course you remember," Bree cajoled. "When a man composes a song for you, you don't forget, even if it's not Shakespeare."

Cassie's face grew warm. She remembered the song very well, but she didn't want her family making a big deal of it. It didn't mean anything…did it? "Okay. He…he called it 'Cassandra's Song.'"

"That's appropriate," Frannie said. "Now sing it for us."

Cassie drew in a breath and softly, tentatively sang the words. "'Cassandra, my Cassandra, like wildflowers in spring, like stars in velvet skies, you are my everything. Cassandra, my Cassandra, your smile warms my heart. We'll sing like this forever, never more to part.'"

"Oh, it is romantic, I knew it!" Bree cried. "Sing the rest of it."

"That's all there is. He said there should be at least another verse, but he didn't have time to write any more."

Her father winked. "Maybe next time, muffin."

"Daddy, stop acting like Antonio and I are… involved. Like I said, we're just friends."

"But there's always the possibility of more."

"No, Daddy, I'm not looking for more. I have too much going on in my life to get distracted by a man."

"But what if he's the man God has for you?" Bree asked.

Cassie sipped her coffee. It was lukewarm now, and too sweet. In her firmest voice she said, "I told you, I'm not looking for a man."

Frannie leaned over and touched Cassie's hand. "Listen, sis, all men aren't like Drake Cameron."

The dining room rang with an awkward silence. The words *Drake Cameron* echoed in the air like a death knell. Cassie's mouth went dry and a sickening knot clenched her stomach.

"I'm sorry, Cass," Frannie said quickly. "I know you don't like us mentioning Drake. But someone has to say something. You can't live your whole life in the shadow of one man who betrayed you."

"This isn't about Drake or anyone else," Cassie retorted. "I'm just not interested in a relationship with anybody right now. Is that a crime?"

"Of course not, Cass. I feel the same way. No romantic entanglements for any of us...until we're good and ready. And that means no more match-making. Agreed?" Her father handed her the platter of hotcakes. "Have another pancake, Cass. Get 'em while they're hot." He gazed around the table at his other daughters. "How about it, girls? Is someone going to demolish these or do I have to polish them off myself?"

After breakfast, as Cassie cleared the table and helped with the dishes, the phrase *no romantic en-*

tanglements drummed in her mind. Surely she had meant what she said about no men in her life, and yet why did thoughts of Antonio steal into her mind when she least expected them? Why did she find herself dreaming of him, and wondering how his kisses would taste, and what it would feel like to be held in his arms? So what if he was handsome and gallant and smart and talented and had a voice that could melt ice and a laugh like music and a smile that reached all the way down to her toes?

Distractedly she put the last china cups and saucers in the dishwasher, poured soap in the dispenser and turned it on. The sudden gushing, churning sound startled her. She had been moving on automatic, her thoughts still on Antonio.

Heaven help her, she couldn't be falling for him like some starry-eyed schoolgirl! Hadn't she been hurt enough by Drake? Hadn't he made a fool of her and cured her of all her romantic notions? Surely she knew better than to get swept up in another doomed liaison!

The phone was ringing. Thank goodness, a distraction! She grabbed the cordless phone from its wall perch and said a bright hello. But the voice on the other end momentarily stole her breath. "Cassandra? Is that you?"

"Antonio?"

"Yes. I hope it's not too early to call."

She moved out of the kitchen into the living room, away from listening ears. "No, it's fine. We just finished breakfast. We're all early risers around here."

"I thought so. I wanted to catch you before you left the house and got busy with your day."

"Well, you caught me."

"Good. I just wanted to thank you for dinner last night. My mother and I had a wonderful time."

Pleasure warmed Cassie's face. "I'm glad. My dad and I had a good time, too."

There was a noticeable moment of silence. Was Antonio waiting for her to say something more? She said the first thing that came to mind. "We'll have to do it again sometime."

"Yes, I'd like that." Antonio's voice was suddenly animated. "In fact, I'd like to show my appreciation, Cassandra. Would you have dinner with me tonight?"

She drew in a sharp breath. Her mind went blank. What was she supposed to do today, tonight?

"Are you free, Cassandra?"

"Yes, I suppose I am. Where would you—"

"I have commitments all day, but I could meet you at a little bistro near my house about six. The Pacific Grille on Prospect. It's nothing fancy, but it's quiet and out of the way, and it has the most beautiful view of the ocean. Truth is, it's one of my favorite places."

"I'm sure I'll love it."

"Then I'll see you there at six." A pause. "Oh, and Cassandra, after all the old camp songs we sang last night, I can't seem to get 'Swanee River' out of my head. It's driving me to distraction."

She laughed in spite of herself. "I know. For me,

it's 'Dixie.' I woke up with it playing in my mind. Over and over and over.''

He joined her laughter. "Then I don't feel so bad. Maybe this evening we can figure out a way to exorcise those tunes from our brains.''

She was still laughing. "That's quite a challenge, but I think I'm up for it.''

"Wonderful. See you tonight.''

Cassie quietly replaced the receiver in its cradle and hurried upstairs before her father or sisters could bombard her with questions. After all of her protestations about not wanting another man in her life, she would hardly appear credible if they knew she had already accepted another date.

That evening Cassie arrived at the restaurant shortly before six. The Pacific Grille was an intriguing single-story log structure resembling a fort, with bottle-glass windows on the street side and wide panels of glass on the ocean side. The dining rooms were small, cozy and dimly lit with lanterns and kerosene lamps. Fishing gear, tackle and nets decorated the lounge area and a massive stuffed swordfish hung over the rough-hewn oyster bar.

Antonio was waiting inside for her, dressed in a casual sport shirt and slacks, his wavy black hair looking attractively windblown. She wondered if she was overdressed in her green knit empire dress and matching three-inch pumps. She relaxed when he greeted her with an approving smile and a light kiss on the cheek that caught her unawares. "You look lovely, Cassandra,'' he whispered as the hostess led them to a small table overlooking the ocean.

"I see why you like it here," she said after the waitress had taken their order—mahi mahi for her, grilled calamari for him—and brought them crystal goblets of sparkling cider. "The ocean feels so close, we could be out to sea."

"That's why I love it…that feeling that you can come here and be anonymous, just you and the lapping waves and the moonlight. And their food is remarkable, too. Of course, not as good as your sister's spaghetti."

Cassie chuckled. "That goes without saying."

He sipped his drink. "I must confess, Cassandra, I don't do this sort of thing very often."

"What thing?"

"Presume upon a lady's generosity two nights in a row."

"But you're not presuming. You invited me to dine with you. I'd call that 'returning the favor,' which is a very gentlemanly thing to do."

He grinned, his dark eyes crinkling at the corners. "I'm glad you see it that way. But still, you were surprised?"

"Surprised? Yes, I suppose so."

"But you knew we would get together again. To practice for the crusade."

"Yes, of course." Cassie winced inwardly. "Is that what this is? You were planning to get some practice in tonight?"

"No, not at all." He sat forward intently, his elbows on the table. "No, tonight is pure pleasure. We're here to have fun. It's just that I'm not accustomed to…to…"

"Having fun?"

"Especially with such a charming young lady. My mother would say I am guilty of immersing myself in my work and my music to the detriment of my social life."

Cassie nodded. "My father accuses me of the same thing."

"Then we must prove them wrong. We must throw caution to the wind and behave like adventurous children."

She laughed. "I'm not sure I remember how."

"Nor do I," he confessed with a droll little smile.

The waitress brought their tossed salads and a basket of rolls. Antonio pulled back the linen cloth and offered Cassie one, then picked up the thread of their conversation. "But last night, my dear Cassandra, when we were laughing together and singing all those silly old songs, I felt freer and happier than I've felt in years."

She met his gaze. "So did I, Antonio."

He reached across the table for her hand and clasped it firmly. "Good! I hoped you did. I guess I wanted to recapture that feeling as quickly as possible. I didn't want to wait another day. I had to find out if we could experience that magic again. Whatever it was. Whatever elusive elixir it might be. I had to know whether just being with a certain person can make a man...me...feel different about himself, about life, about everything."

"I don't know, Antonio. Are you expecting too much? I'm afraid I could never measure up to...to whatever rose-colored image you have in mind."

"But you felt it last night, didn't you? We brought out the best in each other. In every way we played off each other brilliantly. The repartee, the songs, the little jokes. I've never laughed so much in my life, Cassandra. You make me laugh. No one has ever made me laugh."

She extricated her hand from his and ran her fingertips lightly over the fine hairs on his wrist. "You can't be serious, Antonio. You never laugh?"

"Ask my mother what a serious, solitary man I am. Ask my students."

"But I saw you perform. You're one of the most charming, charismatic performers I've ever seen."

"Onstage, yes. It is real, not false. I love my audience. I woo them. I embrace them in my heart. That heady exultation is what I experience onstage." His voice deepened. "But off stage, I feel myself close back up and become...a hermit, a recluse, a man with a lock on his heart. I resist familiarity. I shun the intrusiveness of the crowds. I sometimes yearn to be invisible. Or to barricade myself behind a wall. Does that sound absurd? Eccentric? It's the truth."

Cassie was silent, remembering the rumors she'd heard... *Everyone says Antonio Pagliarulo is mysterious, arrogant, reclusive, aloof...*

"See? I am right. You don't answer me. That means you agree."

"It means no such thing," she protested. "I was just thinking about what you said, how poignant and compelling your words are." She nibbled a morsel of roll. "I've been onstage enough to sense that same euphoria of performing, of feeling the audience with you, lifting you up, until you almost feel you're courting them.''

"Yes, of course you would know that!"

"But I don't think I've experienced the dichotomy you describe. Feeling the closeness, the intimacy with an audience, and then retreating, erecting a wall, feeling distant, remote. You're an enigma, a paradox, Mr. Pagliarulo.''

He broke off a crust of sourdough bread. "Then I hope I have whetted your curiosity, Cassandra. Because when I am with you I feel the strange compunction to divulge my most private self, to pour out my secret heart. It's an unsettling sensation, and I'm not quite sure how to deal with it. I hope my candor doesn't offend you.''

"Offend me? On the contrary. I value honesty in a relationship above all else.'' The shadowed image of Drake flashed in her mind. Drake's terrible pretenses and lies. Drake crushing her love with his deceit. "Anything less is a disservice,'' she said with conviction. "Anything less than the truth is betrayal.''

"I believe that, too, Cassandra.'' Gently he enveloped her slim hand in his large one. "But rarely does one find a person one can be scrupulously honest with…that giving, guileless woman to whom a man can bare his very soul.''

For an instant Cassie couldn't quite breathe, couldn't pull her gaze from Antonio's warm, riveting eyes, or quiet the sudden pounding of her heart. If it were possible for a woman to sense the very second her affection for a man blossomed into the sweet delirium of love, she would have to confess this was that rare, electrifying moment.

Chapter Eight

After dinner, Cassie and Antonio walked down by the beach just beyond the Pacific Grille's sloping bluff. Cassie could still hear the strains of a romantic ballad wafting from the restaurant. A cool October wind was stirring, crisp and refreshing, scenting the air with a moist, briny tang. The stars were bright and the moonlight cast a luminous glow over the tide's foamy whitecaps. The ocean's steady roar sounded in Cassie's ears like a comforting background motif.

Antonio caught her hand and swung it as they walked. He looked over at her with a grin, the moonlight accenting his chiseled features. "Are we going to do this up right, Cassandra?"

"Right? What do you mean?"

"Well, if we're going to play in the sand...if we're going to be bold and reckless...then there's only one way to walk on a beach." He released her hand, stooped down and removed his shoes and socks, and proceeded to roll up his pant legs. "If you laugh, Cassandra, you're in trouble."

She stifled a giggle. "I won't. I promise." She kicked off her pumps and wriggled her bare toes in the heavy, wet sand. It felt good, invigorating.

Antonio seized her hand again. "Now for the next step."

"There's another step?"

"Of course. Come on!" He broke into a run toward the inrushing waves. "Let's get our feet wet!"

She ran beside him, laughing, the moist air filling her nostrils, her lungs. Goose bumps prickled on her arms and the breeze sent her perfect curls into a free-falling cascade. They waded into the rippling waves until the chilly water was up to their calves. "Be careful, Antonio. One wrong step and we'll be drenched."

Antonio paused and faced her and clasped her bare arms just above the elbows. He was breathing deeply, a smile playing on his lips. "Cassandra, has anyone ever told you how lovely you look standing in the ocean, with the moonlight turning your skin to satin and the wind transforming your hair into a golden waterfall?"

She caught her breath. "My dear Mr. Pagliarulo, has anyone told you, you have the makings of a poet?"

Antonio laughed and held up a dripping foot. "No, but my Longfellow feet sure show it!"

"Oh, that's such an ancient joke!"

He ruffled her hair. "Don't be cruel. After all, I

can't be all things…a minstrel…a poet…a comedian.''

She placed her palms lightly on his chest and said softly, "Oh, yes. You can be anything you choose, Antonio.''

He ran his finger gently over her cheek, her chin, his sable eyes searching hers. "You almost make me believe that, Cassandra.''

She shivered.

He ran his hands over her arms. "You're cold. I'd better get you back to the car. We can't have you catching pneumonia.''

She waved him off. "I'm fine. It was just a chill from the wind.''

"Well, enough playing. I think I've indulged my inner child enough for one night.''

Before she realized what he was doing, Antonio swept her up in his arms and carried her out of the water and across the dark expanse of beach. She bristled, about to protest. Then she realized how good his strong arms felt around her, as if they had been made to hold her.

He cradled her against his chest for several moments, with only the sound of his breathing blending with the distant crashing waves. He looked down at her, his solemn face cast in shadows like a Michelangelo sculpture, and then slowly he lowered his face to hers and moved his lips tenderly over hers.

Instinctively she responded, returning the kiss. The moment was magical, a dream, unreal, dazzling and dizzying. She had never felt this way with any man—not even with Drake—this sweet ecstasy of devotion and desire. Everything was different, changed. She would never look at Antonio the same way again. Did he feel it too, this glorious, delicious, rollicking emotion?

At last he set her down and they padded over and picked up their shoes. Neither spoke as he walked her to her car. He waited while she fished in her purse for her key. "I don't want this evening to end," he said quietly. "Once you drive away I'll turn back into a sane, rational man again, a dull reflection of who I am when I'm with you."

She smiled up at him. "I feel the same way. I'm the most practical, conservative person I know. But with you I feel as if I could be anything, anyone."

He knuckled her chin. "I think that means we're good for each other."

She unlocked her door.

"No, don't go yet, Cassandra. We can't just fritter away magic like this." He looked at his watch. "I figure we've got at least an hour before this vehicle turns into a pumpkin."

She laughed. "And what do you turn into, Antonio?"

He walked his fingers lightly up her arm. "Why don't you stay and find out?"

She shivered again. Was it the cold? Or his electrifying presence? "What should we do? Go back into the restaurant? Order dessert?"

"Or we could just sit here together in your automobile, like teenagers, and I could hold you in my arms to keep you warm. And we could talk until that whole midnight-pumpkin thing happens."

She nodded. "That's better than any dessert."

She climbed in the driver's seat while he went around to the passenger's side. When they were settled, he slipped his arm around her and drew her close. She relaxed her head on his shoulder and felt safe and warm and protected. And cherished. Yes, that was it. She felt cherished. What a priceless sensation!

"Are you warm enough now?" he asked, his mouth moving against her ear.

"Perfect. But I keep thinking I'm going to wake up and marvel at what a sweet dream this has been."

"If it's just a dream, I hope we don't wake up for a long time."

She looked up at him. "Tell me, Antonio. How did we go from being friends...good, companionable friends...to this...whatever this is?"

He shrugged. "Would you believe I'm as surprised by this delightful turn of events as you are?"

She chuckled. "Great! We're a fine pair. We stumbled into something neither of us saw coming. What does that say about us?"

"A match made in heaven, as they say?"

She searched his eyes. "I don't know, Antonio. Are we? We still hardly know each other." Her fingertips gently grazed his jaw. "But there's so much I want to know about you."

He pressed her hand against his cheek. "And I want to know everything about you."

She nestled closer to him. "There's not much to tell. I've been consumed with my music since I was a little girl."

"What about the men in your life?"

She was silent for a long moment.

"What about the man who hurt you?"

"A few years ago there was a man, but I try not to think about him anymore."

"I'm listening...if you feel like talking."

She cleared her throat uneasily. "It was the summer after I'd received my degree at Juilliard. I was taking some graduate courses at UCLA. An assistant professor began pursuing me. I was flattered and charmed. He was an older man, cultured, sophisticated, clever." Cassie twisted her watch band, her agitation rising as the memories flooded back. "Drake swept me off my feet and made grand promises, and I fell hopelessly in love. At least, I assumed it was love."

"Love takes many forms, many faces."

"And his was the face of betrayal."

"What happened, Cassandra?" Antonio pressed gently.

"One night I stopped by his office at the university to see if he wanted to go out to dinner. It was just a spontaneous idea, a lark. But I was too late. A woman and little girl were already waiting for him. We chatted a few minutes and slowly it dawned on me." Cassie's voice wavered. "These were his wife and daughter, and the three of them were about to go out to celebrate the child's birthday."

Antonio's arm tightened around Cassie. "I'm sorry, Cassandra. How painful that must have been."

Tears brimmed in her eyes. "I felt dirty, like a homewrecker. It hadn't occurred to me that he was married. I promised myself I would never make such a mistake again. To be sure I wouldn't, I haven't dated anyone seriously since Drake.''

Antonio nuzzled her hair. ''Not all men are scoundrels.''

She looked up at him. ''Thank God for that.''

''Thank God He has brought us together, Cassandra. I don't know what lies ahead, but I sense that something extraordinary is happening between us. Something that perhaps God Himself has ordained.''

Cassie's voice came out soft, breathy. ''I vowed never to give my heart to anyone again....''

''And now?''

''I don't know, Antonio. Perhaps in time...''

''Yes. Time. And I'm afraid it is almost time for that pumpkin....''

''No fair. I've done all the talking. You haven't told me anything.''

He kissed her ear. ''What do you want to know?''

''I don't know. Everything. What were you like as a child? What were your parents like? I mean, I know your mother now, but what was she like then?''

''Oh, you don't really want me to get into all of that tonight.''

''Yes, I do. Please. Tell me about your parents.''

Antonio drummed his fingers on her arm. ''My parents? All right, you asked for it. They were both in the theater. My father was a good deal older than my mother. He was an actor and singer. He performed in little theater and off-Broadway plays.''

''How exciting. And your mother?''

''My mother was just a teenager when they met.

Not quite sixteen. She had run away from home and was trying to break into the theater. My father heard her sing at an audition and was enraptured by her beauty and her voice."

"Did he know how young she was?"

"No. She told him she was eighteen, and he believed her. In fact, he helped her get a small role in the chorus of a Broadway musical. They fell in love while performing together in several plays."

"What a perfect story-book romance."

"Yes, I suppose it seemed so at first. She was only seventeen when they married. I was born a year later."

"Did they continue to perform together?"

"Yes. And they dragged me along to the theater from the time I was a tiny tot. I grew up amid the greasepaint and costumes and flashing lights. The scenery props were my playrooms. The actors and musicians were my surrogate parents."

"Oh, Antonio, tell me about it."

His voice grew wistful. "My first memories are of sitting in the wings watching my parents perform and wanting desperately to run out onstage to be with them. They seemed to be having such a marvelous time. They were playacting in colorful clothes and stunning sets, the very thing every child dreams of doing. At least I did. But of course the propman or costume director or whoever my mother persuaded to watch me held me back and kept me quiet with a lollipop or a theater program to color on."

"It sounds like something out of a fairy tale."

"It was. I adored my parents. Onstage, they were so full of energy and life. Bigger than life."

Cassie smiled up at him. "It must have been a magical childhood!"

Antonio's lips tightened and his brows furrowed. "At times like those, it was. But then the play always ended and my parents packed me up and took me home."

"What…what happened then?"

He inhaled deeply, his chest shuddering slightly. "My father was a very talented, impassioned man, Cassandra. But he never managed to achieve the success my mother attained. It was strange. Somehow his career grew stagnant while hers flourished. He began staying home while my mother went off to the theater to perform. How I dreaded those times."

"Why?"

"Because he was always so angry, so brooding and withdrawn. He turned to the bottle and began to drink heavily."

"I'm so sorry."

Antonio's voice thickened with contempt. "My father became an alcoholic. His drinking made him lose even the occasional minor roles and the small acclaim he still possessed. My mother's triumphs only fueled the fires for him, driving him deeper into drink. He ended up eking out a living by giving singing lessons to neighborhood children."

"But you told me he died when you were quite young."

"Yes. I was ten." Antonio gazed out the window, his tone growing distant, detached. "We were on vacation in the Catskill Mountains when our car plunged over a cliff. My father was killed instantly."

Cassie reached over and turned Antonio's face back to hers and searched his eyes. "And you never had a chance to resolve your feelings about your father, did you?"

"I suppose not. I loved him and I hated him...with equal intensity. And I will feel guilty for his death for as long as I live."

"But why? You were a child. You had nothing to do with it. It wasn't your fault."

Antonio stiffened and moved his arm to the back of the seat, his mood changing abruptly. "I don't know how we got into this, but we have definitely used up our borrowed time. And if this car isn't about to become a pumpkin, I am certainly about to change into an old workhorse or a vile rat or some other obnoxious creature."

She laughed mirthlessly. "Antonio, you'll do no such thing."

"Are you saying I shall never be anything but your charming and gallant prince?"

"I didn't say that." She looked at her watch, squinting through the shadows. "You're right. It is getting late. The bewitching hour. I'd better go before my father or your mother calls out the militia."

He leaned over, cupped her chin in his hand and planted a warm kiss on her forehead. "It's been a beautiful evening. We'll do this again...soon."

"And I'll see you at rehearsal," she called after him as he stepped out of the car. Why did she have a sinking feeling they might never be this close again, or never quite recapture this magic? "Don't forget. The crusade is only two weeks away."

He gazed back inside her open door. "How could I forget? We have a lot of work to do before then. And don't forget what brought us together in the first place!"

Her mind was blank. "What?"

He grinned impishly. "Our little plot to bring our parents together. To help them find a little enjoyment and companionship. Have you forgotten? It was your idea!"

She laughed self-consciously. "Of course I haven't forgotten. Just give me time. We'll think of something."

He blew her a kiss. "For now, good night, dear heart."

She watched as he walked to his car, her eyes fastened on his broad shoulders, lean physique and long, striding legs. In one evening he had reduced her to a lovesick schoolgirl. Her thoughts were reeling, skittering like fireflies in a bottle. She couldn't begin to think of hapless matchmaking schemes when all she wanted was to remain in Antonio's warm and sturdy arms.

Chapter Nine

The weekend was over and Andrew was in a mood…contemplative, a bit melancholy, a tad restless. He couldn't pinpoint the feeling exactly, but it was pronounced enough that he couldn't ignore it, either. Even on this warm October morning, he felt a shadow over his soul. After his daughters had gone their various ways—Cassie to the university, Brianna to her counseling center and Frannie to the sunroom to work on her sculpture—Andrew lingered at the kitchen table over a second cup of coffee.

He could blame his blue mood on the fact that it was Monday morning and he was always physically weary and emotionally spent after a full day of Sunday preaching. But this was more than a passing attack of the doldrums. He felt a heaviness in his soul, an ache he couldn't reach. It wouldn't go away.

Finally, his agitation growing, Andrew picked up his cup of coffee and trudged upstairs to his bedroom retreat. Maybe he would even sit out on the balcony and soak up a little sun. He grabbed his Bible from the nightstand and headed out onto the cozy balcony. He settled in one of the two pine chairs—one was Mandy's but he could never bring himself to remove it—and set his coffee on the small pedestal table.

He opened his Bible on his lap and scanned a few passages, but he couldn't get the words off the page. His mind was too distracted this morning, like leaves scattered in an autumn wind. He already suspected what the trouble was. He was spending too much time lately with Juliana, and her presence—her ruby smile, her roses-and-raspberry smell, her husky voice and bountiful laughter—had a way of reminding him what he had lost when Mandy died. When there was no woman in his life, he could manage to block out the memories of Mandy.

But Juliana was stirring something deep and familiar in his soul—memories of what it was like to feel a woman's warmth beside him when he woke in the morning, memories of intimate, whispered conversations in the dark, memories of making love with the one woman on earth who knew him inside out and loved him anyway.

Andrew was in a dilemma. Should he banish Juliana from his life or eagerly embrace her? He wanted to do both. Push her away so the memories would stop? Or take her in his arms and give expression to the youthful passions he had almost forgotten? But that wouldn't be fair to Juliana, for he couldn't be sure whether he truly cared about her or saw her as a convenient, if unlikely, substitute for his beloved Mandy.

"Mandy, oh Mandy," he said aloud, with an edge of desperation, "what am I supposed to do?" The question was left hanging in a heavy silence. Usually when he talked to Mandy like this, he felt a sense of camaraderie, as if she were somehow still here, listening, sympathizing, sharing his burdens. But this morning he felt only a vacuum, a strange void, as if his wispy memory of Mandy had withdrawn, vanished.

The idea that Mandy was no longer accessible to him even on the level of pure reminiscence disturbed him more than he was willing to admit. He had been forced to relinquish his wife on so many levels—physical, spiritual, emotional. Now even those gauzy, gossamer images of Mandy in his imagination were slipping away. Sometimes lately when he tried to recall her serene face, it was Juliana's glowing, laughing features he saw instead.

What guilt that stirred!

He rubbed his hand over his wide jaw. "Lord, I'm an old fool, aren't I? Won't let go even when I know she's gone. Scared out of my wits to get too close to someone else. Scared I might feel something again, and heaven help me, what would I do then? I'm too set in my ways to go off the deep end, Lord, and get all moonstruck over a woman I hardly know."

Sometimes Andrew felt like a phony. He was known for his good humor, his exuberance, his good nature. He knew how to put on a good show for his congregation; he knew the right words to say when

a parishioner was hurting or in trouble or facing a
crisis. He had said the words long enough that they
came out automatically with an ease and sincerity
that convinced others they were heartfelt.

And they were...to a point. But what no one knew,
no, not even his darling daughters, was that the emotions behind the words and actions had long since
withered and died. Not the surface emotions. He
could manufacture those easily enough. But when
Mandy died, something crucial died in Andrew,
too—the ability to feel deep emotion.

Andrew closed his Bible and ran his palm over the
worn leather cover. He loved this book, taught it, fed
on it, lived by it. There was a time when just reading
these God-breathed words brought tears to his eyes;
a time when he could sit in God's presence and weep
for what Christ had done for him on the cross, the
sacrificial love that had driven Jesus to die an excru-
ciating death, counting it all joy to redeem humanity.

But it had been years now since Andrew had wept
over his sins, or shed tears over another's pain, or
sobbed on his face for a lost and broken world. In
his youth, those urgent, ardent emotions had compelled him to enter the ministry, had infused his
preaching with a warmth and vitality the Spirit had
used to make his work flourish.

But what worried Andrew most of all these days
was the possibility that his tender, intimate walk with
the Lord had suffered since Mandy's death. Was he
more guarded now with God, knowing his Heavenly
Father could extract such a heavy price from

him…even his beloved wife? What next? One of his precious daughters?

Andrew constantly reassured himself that he was not angry with God. He knew many people facing loss cried out, "Why me, God?" But Andrew was wise enough, rationally minded enough, to concede, "Why not me, God?" He took an almost adverse pride in his ability to keep a stiff upper lip, to accept his loss and go on with dignity and gentle good humor.

But sometimes Andrew felt guilty preaching to his congregation, telling them how to face their struggles—the myriad hurts, adversities and temptations that assaulted them. Some with troubled marriages, some out of work, some in destructive relationships. He presumed to counsel these dear people about life, and yet he himself had withdrawn emotionally from his own life. A crucial part of him remained detached, uninvolved.

How could he tell others what to do when he himself wasn't willing to get in there and fight and let himself feel again, let himself experience all the raw, messy, paradoxical emotions that seize a person when he swings open his heart and mind to them? How could he tell them God could be their all in all, the answer to every need, when a part of himself was still raw and tender, when he kept that central feeling part of himself caged away, like a wild animal that might bolt and wreak havoc if he allowed it to run free?

Andrew set his Bible down and reached for his coffee. He liked sitting on his balcony. From his private little perch he could see the world around him...the other yards and houses, the distant mountains, the cloud-studded sky. He could smell the ocean and hear the birds sing, could even hear the distant freeway traffic sounding like a gentle purr. Here in the privacy of his balcony he could brood or indulge his melancholy moods without having to explain himself to his daughters. Here he could speak frankly with God, one on one, face-to-face, so to speak. But he wasn't sure he was up to squaring off with the Almighty this morning.

He sipped his coffee and grimaced. It was cold now, so he set the cup down beside his Bible. "Lord," he said aloud, his voice sounding small, lost in sunlight and air, "I fall so far short of Your glory. I know that's why You reached down to us—heaven help us, we couldn't reach high enough to You. At moments like this I'm mighty glad Your Son spanned the gap. Stretched His arms out on a cross and gave us grace. I need it today, Lord, Your unmerited favor, Your love."

Andrew sat forward and put his face in his hands and rubbed his temples. "Lord, I'm not a very good example of Your Son. When He walked this earth, He took on the hurts of the people He loved, let Himself feel their pain, became their pain." Andrew's voice grew husky, his throat tight. "God, I feel as if I've closed myself up, as if I'm watching from a distance. I don't let myself feel my people's heartaches anymore. I'm not even sure I recognize my own. Help me, God. I'm losing something important in myself, and I don't even know what it is."

Andrew stood up and stretched, the muscles in his shoulders tense. He didn't seem to have any words left. Maybe it was time to stop talking and start doing. Maybe he needed to confront Juliana and break off this thing between them before it even began. All right, it had begun—something was there—but it was still fragile enough that it could be nipped in the bud. Then maybe he could get his life back in order.

He would phone her and invite her to get together to talk. He would be as tactful as possible and maybe she would be as relieved as he to sever any potential romantic entanglement. But why telephone and risk her saying no and thus postponing the inevitable? He would get in his car and drive directly to her house; he would show up on her doorstep and they would settle this now, once and for all.

Andrew stopped by the sunroom to kiss Frannie goodbye and compliment her on her work; he grabbed the address book from the junk drawer in the kitchen, and paused in the foyer long enough to give Ruggs a good scratch behind the ears. Then he was off on his fateful mission.

It took less than twenty minutes to drive to the Pagliarulo estate on a bluff overlooking the Pacific. A sprawling, two-story white stucco mansion with Roman pillars and a red-tile roof sat ensconced on a manicured lawn festooned with towering palms and eucalyptus trees, with a panoramic view of the ocean. It was breathtaking. Two stone lions guarded a wide, redbrick walkway that led up to the house.

As Andrew strode up the walkway to the spacious porch, he reminded himself why he was paying Juliana this visit. Surely she would understand that people of their age and station in life needed to exert certain precautions. It would be foolish for them to run headlong into an emotional involvement when their lives were already pleasantly settled and comfortably predictable. Surely she would understand his reasoning and not take offense. After all, he wasn't rejecting her; he was just forestalling the risk of a regrettable misadventure.

With his resolve renewed, Andrew knocked soundly on the carved double doors. After a long minute, the door opened and Juliana stood framed in the doorway staring up at him in astonishment. In form-fitting jeans and a silk blouse tied at the waist, she looked like a young girl with no makeup, her ebony hair cascading over her slim shoulders. She was stunning. "Andrew! What are you doing here?"

All of his sensible resolves dissolved as he gazed at her. He was speechless. He mumbled something about being in the neighborhood, which was as close as he had come lately to uttering an untruth. She obviously saw through his bumbling explanation, but was kind enough not to challenge him. "Come in, Andrew," she said, stepping back into her marble foyer. "It's good to see you."

"Good to see you, too, Juliana," he murmured as he followed her inside. Her home was enormous, with ten-foot ceilings, a circular oak staircase, crystal chandeliers and ornamental moldings and woodwork. While sunlight spilled in through an abundance of windows, the tasteful cherry wood furnishings and ornate Renaissance-style paintings gave the house an Old World European ambiance.

"It's beautiful," Andrew said, gazing around.

"Thank you. Antonio and I have managed to blend our tastes and styles quite nicely." She led him through the living and dining rooms to a comfortable family room with overstuffed sofas and ceiling-to-floor bookcases. "Could I get you some tea? A sandwich? A Danish?"

He sat down on a sofa facing a massive stone fireplace. "No, I'm fine, Juliana. Maybe coffee. Or tea. Whatever. Don't go to any trouble."

"No trouble. Is instant okay?"

"Sure. And maybe the Danish, after all. Never could refuse a good Danish."

She smiled. "Fine. I'll be right back." She returned minutes later with a silver platter with delicate china teacups and a plate of fancy pastries. She set the platter on the coffee table and handed him a steaming cup of black coffee. "Sugar?" she asked.

"What?"

"Sugar. Do you take sugar? Cream?"

"No, black is okay." He sipped the coffee, but it was too hot, so he set the cup back on the table.

Juliana offered him a fancy china plate containing small pastries drizzled with white icing. He gingerly selected one and took a nibble. It was too sticky and flaky for polite consumption. He took another bite, knowing he was destined to make a mess. Luckily he wasn't wearing his black suit. Hopefully the crumbs wouldn't show on his casual sport shirt and tan slacks.

Juliana sat down on the sofa beside him and gave him a bemused look. "It's quite tasty, isn't it, Andrew?"

He nodded. Maybe the secret was to eat the entire confection in one hearty mouthful. He popped the remaining portion of the delicacy into his mouth and immediately regretted it. The pastry was too sweet, too rich and too large to chew and swallow discreetly. But he had no choice. Juliana was watching him expectantly. No doubt she had baked these beauties with her own precious little fingers. He didn't dare insult her culinary skills when he was already about to lower the boom on any future relationship.

After an agonizing few moments Andrew swallowed the last of his pastry and gave a sigh of relief. Juliana was still watching him. "Would you like another?" she asked with her usual beaming smile.

He waved her off. "No, that was, uh, remarkable, but no more. Watching my waistline, you know."

"You have a marvelous waistline," she said with a teasing little laugh.

Andrew chuckled self-consciously. "And that's how I keep my trim figure, by refusing seconds. Of everything except spaghetti, of course."

"Of course." Unexpectedly Juliana leaned close and ran a polished fingernail over the side of his mouth. "Crumbs," she explained.

His face flushing with sudden warmth, Andrew removed a handkerchief from his trousers pocket and wiped his mouth. "Guess I should have brought one of Frannie's bibs."

Juliana broke into spontaneous laughter. "Yes,

you should have. You should keep one in the car for occasions like this.''

''I'll remember next time.''

Juliana studied him intently, a smile gracing her lips. ''Tell me now, Andrew. Don't be coy. What is your reason for dropping by?''

''My reason?'' His mind was blank. Everything had seemed so clear to him earlier this morning, but now... ''I—I thought perhaps we should have a little talk. Express our concerns.''

''Concerns?''

''Not concerns exactly. It's just...we've seen each other several times now, and I thought...before we go any further...''

''Yes, Andrew?''

''I thought perhaps we needed an understanding. Take two steps back perhaps. Clarify our positions. Or maybe I'm being too presumptuous.'' He gazed miserably at her, knowing he was digging the hole deeper and deeper. ''I don't suppose you have the slightest idea what I'm talking about.''

She shook her head. ''I'm sorry, Andrew. Perhaps you should come right out and say what's on your mind.''

He stood up abruptly and walked over to the nearest bookcase. He was running like a lily-livered coward. With sweating palms, he scanned the rows of hardback volumes as if he were actually looking for something.

Juliana came over and stood beside him. ''Are you looking for a particular title?''

He quickly shook his head. ''No, I just enjoy perusing people's libraries. Never know what you'll find." *Lord, what am I doing here?* he begged silently. *Get me out of this!*

Slowly, leisurely, borrowing time, he ran his fingertips over several thick tomes—history, music, art, Shakespeare, great composers, famous operas; it was all here, any subject a cultural person might fancy. Finally, almost instinctively, Andrew removed a slender leather-bound book and flipped it open. There was something familiar about its tissue-thin pages, something mysteriously compelling.

Then it struck him like a dagger to the heart. It was a collection of Emily Dickinson's poems. Mandy's favorite poet. She had memorized nearly every poem in this very book and had often recited them to him, although at first he had only half listened in accommodating bemusement. He had been too busy with serious, lofty matters to pay attention to quaint little poems.

It was Mandy who had brought him up sharp and taught him to listen with the heart as well as the ear, until the day came when the sound of Mandy's voice reading Emily Dickinson brought tears to his eyes. Mandy quoted Dickinson even when she was dying. Andrew remembered the stanzas as if they had been branded with fire on the tender flesh of his heart.... Dickinson's poem, "After Great Pain," that spoke of letting go, her haunting, unforgettable "Because I Could Not Stop for Death," that echoed Mandy's own dying, and the bitter, final irony of "I Heard a Fly Buzz."

Suddenly it all flooded back—a slamming, pounding inrush of memories staggering him, knocking him off balance, stealing his breath. He was back with Mandy. The end was near. She lay in bed staring at the ceiling, a look in her eyes he couldn't read. Not fear exactly, something deeper, a thing beyond words. He saw it in her eyes; they glittered with a disquieting intensity. It was a profound thing, consuming, an expression not of this earth. She was in a place he couldn't reach, a place where only God could go with her.

How his heart had ached that he couldn't share what she was feeling, couldn't alleviate her pain, couldn't walk with her all the way. He was a man of God and totally helpless in the face of her suffering. Even when he held her fragile body in his arms and wept into her fine, silky hair, he couldn't get close to her, couldn't begin to experience what she was experiencing. They were in two separate worlds, a gulf apart. All he could do was watch and wait, awed by her courage, her quiet dignity.

Now, as he fingered the book of poems, he realized, to his own astonishment, that tears were running down his cheeks. He brushed them away quickly, lest Juliana notice. Too late. She was already reaching her graceful hand out to him, concern written in her forehead, her eyes. "Andrew? Are you all right?"

"Yes, fine. It's nothing. Something in my eye."

"Tears! Andrew, you're crying." She stepped closer, so near her rose-scented perfume wafted in his nostrils. She placed her smooth, warm palm against his wet cheek. "What is it? Did I say something? Oh, Andrew, tell me what's wrong."

"Nothing's wrong. I just...my sinuses...allergies..." He was rambling now, grabbing excuses from the air, making no sense whatsoever.

"Allergies? Are you allergic to something? My perfume? But wouldn't you be sneezing? Not weeping!"

"It's not allergies," he confessed. "I don't know why I said that. I just got choked up. No reason. Just looking at this book of poems and feeling sentimental, I guess."

Juliana looked bewildered. "Poems make you feel sad?"

Almost gruffly, because he didn't want to get into it, Andrew explained, "Emily Dickinson was Mandy's favorite poet."

Juliana pursed her lips, making a sad face. "Oh, dear Andrew, tell me what I can do to help."

"Nothing!" The more of a fuss she made, the worse he felt. He was humiliated, frustrated, angry with himself. He hadn't let anyone see him weep since Mandy died. If he was going to make a blubbering fool of himself, why did it have to be in front of Juliana, of all people? "I've got to go," he said abruptly. He slipped the little volume back into the bookcase and turned on his heel toward the door.

Juliana clasped his arm. "Don't go, Andrew. Not like this. Don't be afraid to let me see your pain." She faced him squarely, reached up and took his face gently in her hands. "You minister to so many people. You help so many. For once, let someone else be strong for you.''

''I don't know what you're talking about,'' he said with forced laughter, as if she had made an outrageous joke. He wanted to sidestep her and get out, but it was as if some force had stolen his breath, his strength, his willpower.

Impulsively Juliana drew close and brushed a kiss against his cheek. Her lips were like butterfly wings, light as air, a gentle flutter, soft as rose petals.

Andrew seized her arms, as if to hold her at a distance. ''Juliana! Don't!'' The words were harsh, visceral, from somewhere deep inside him.

She stared up at him with a wounded, childlike expression. ''I'm sorry, Andrew. I didn't mean to—''

Instinctively, as if something larger than himself compelled him, he gathered Juliana into his arms and kissed her soundly on the lips, unleashing five years of pent-up emotion. She returned the kiss with a warmth and tenderness that only fueled his hunger. He wanted to hold her like this forever, lose himself in the sweetness of her lips.

But somehow, cold reason returned and he relinquished her. ''Juliana, I shouldn't have,'' he stammered, his heart pounding fiercely. ''Forgive me. I had no right...''

She met his gaze unflinchingly. ''You owe me no apology, Andrew, for something I wanted as much as you.''

''But that's not what I intended, Juliana. I came here to—''

Andrew's words were broken by a crashing sound

upstairs, followed by a woman's piercing scream somewhere in the innards of the house. It was an eerie, unearthly sound that sent a chill through his bones. He whirled around. "What in the world—?"

Juliana was already striding past him, her face white with alarm. He followed her back to the living room. "Who was that? Should I phone for help?"

"No, just go, Andrew." Juliana paused for a moment at the foot of the circular staircase and gazed entreatingly at him. There was an odd fire in her eyes and pinched, worried lines in her forehead. "Please, Andrew, I can handle this. Just leave. Let yourself out. I'll call you. Good day!"

Andrew shuffled out the door and let it slam behind him, but once he was in his car and on the way home he chastised himself for not following Juliana upstairs. Someone was obviously in trouble, and by the expression on Juliana's face, she was more than a little upset. Why hadn't he stayed and helped?

Maybe because, as distressed as Juliana was, she obviously didn't want Andrew assisting her. Why? What secret was she hiding? It was a mystery that seemed to grow in disturbing proportions the more Andrew tried to figure it out. He was beginning to realize, as attracted as he was to Juliana Pagliarulo, he really knew very little about her.

Chapter Ten

That same day, Cassie had spent the morning practicing the piano, getting in her usual three hours, and was just about to take a lunch break when the telephone rang. She grabbed the cordless phone in the kitchen as she headed for the refrigerator, and said a quick hello.

There was a pause on the other end, then a remotely familiar voice said, "Cassie, is that you?"

She dropped her hand from the refrigerator door. "Yes. Who is this?"

The voice took on a faintly teasing sound. "Don't you know who this is?"

She gripped the edge of the countertop. Was it possible? Surely not! "Who is this?" she demanded.

"Drake," came the reply she dreaded, yet once secretly yearned for. "Drake Cameron. Cassie, are you still there?"

"Yes, I'm here," she said in a small, hushed

voice. This had to be a dream, a nightmare. "What do you want, Drake?"

He uttered a mirthless chuckle, but his voice was still suave and as smooth as glass. "Just wanted to call and say hello, Cassie. It's been a long time."

A long time indeed! Four years since I told you goodbye, she thought darkly. Four years since I discovered you were a liar and a cheat. "We have nothing to say to each other, Drake."

"Oh, but Cassie, we do. A lot's happened in four years."

"I'm not interested," she said coldly.

"Listen, Cassie, this isn't something we can talk about over the phone. Meet me for a cup of coffee, okay?"

She stiffened, fighting the warring emotions erupting inside her. "No, Drake, I'm busy," she said unevenly. "Don't bother me again."

"Wait, Cassie. Don't hang up!"

She was about to, but she couldn't bring herself to drop the receiver back into its cradle. She waited, praying for the strength to fend off this man she had once hated and loved with equal intensity. "What is it, Drake?" she said at last. "Why are you calling me after all this time?"

"Because I've missed you, Cass." His voice still had that persuasive, disarming quality that made her heart do flip-flops. "I've never gotten you out of my system. You're still there in my head, in my heart."

"This is where we left off, Drake." It was like a broken record, the same old scenario. She couldn't believe he was spewing the same tired banalities.

"You can spout all the sweet talk you want, Drake, but you're a married man, remember? A husband and a father, which you conveniently forgot."

"I'm not forgetting, Cass," he said quickly. "Listen, things have changed for me. I'm divorced now. My wife has our daughter. Full custody. She won't even let me see my little girl."

"That has nothing to do with me, Drake." Cassie drummed her fingers on the ceramic tile counter. "I've really got to go."

"Then you won't see me?"

"No. I—I'm seeing someone else." It wasn't a lie. She was, in a sense, seeing Antonio, even if there was nothing official between them.

Drake sounded unfazed. "I don't care. I'm not giving up, Cassie. We had something good between us once. Don't you see, sweetheart? Now I'm free. We can pick up where we left off."

"No, Drake, don't even think—!" Cassie heard a beep. "Listen, Drake, I've got to go. There's someone on the other line."

"I'll call you again. Think over what I said, Cassie."

Without replying she clicked over to the other line and said hello. A warm, resonant voice said, "Hello, Cassandra."

"Oh, Antonio!" She almost wept with relief.

"Are you all right? You sound distressed."

"No, I'm fine now. It's good to hear your voice."

"I was wondering if you'd like to have dinner with me tonight."

"Dinner?"

"The Pacific Grille. We had such a good time there the other night, I figure it's our place now. A place to build some more memories. What do you say?"

She was beaming like a Cheshire cat. "I'd love to."

"Great. I'll be tied up at the university most of the day. Do you want to meet me there? Say about seven?"

"Seven would be perfect. I'll see you tonight."

For the rest of the day, as Cassie ran errands and taught a late-afternoon class at the university, she felt giddy, flushed, distracted, as if she were wafting about on a cloud of chiffon, anticipating a tiny bit of heaven. Imagine! She would be spending the evening with Antonio again. Dear Antonio, a man of honor and integrity.

How thankful she was that God had brought him into her life just when she might have been tempted to see Drake again. God knew what He was doing. He had brought a new love into her life in the nick of time. With thoughts of Antonio swirling in her head, there would be no room for the likes of Drake Cameron.

That evening, Cassie left early for the Pacific Grille. On the way she checked for messages on her cell phone and was surprised to find one from Antonio. He said simply, "Cass, something urgent has come up. I won't be able to meet you at the Pacific Grille tonight. I'm sorry. I'll call you later to set a date for another time."

Disappointment washed over her as she closed her

cell phone and slipped it into her purse. She had counted so much on this date with Antonio. It was to have been the perfect evening to expel any remnant feelings she carried for Drake Cameron. Aloud she said, "Whatever called you away, Antonio, it must have been terribly important, because I know this date meant a lot to you, too."

She was about to turn around and drive home when she realized she was only a matter of minutes from the restaurant. In a rush of nostalgia, she decided to drive on to the Pacific Grille and have dinner there anyway. Just sitting by those panoramic windows overlooking the ocean would remind her of the special moments she had shared with Antonio...their cozy dinner, their walk on the beach, his tender kiss.

She pulled into the parking lot and for a moment wondered if she was being ridiculous to go in and eat alone. Perhaps she should have driven home and waited until she could experience this unique place with Antonio again. But no, she was here now. Might as well go inside.

She entered the quaint fortlike building with its bottle-glass windows and kerosene lamps and waited for a hostess to seat her. As her eyes grew accustomed to the shadowed room with its flickering lanterns, she began to distinguish the various tables and their patrons. One couple drew her attention. The man was a dead ringer for Antonio.

She took a few steps off to one side to catch another view of the man, and her heart caught in her throat. There was no mistake. It was Antonio Pagliarulo sitting at a corner table with a young brunette woman. Her long raven-black hair flowed loosely over one eye and cheekbone so that only half of her face showed. But from what Cassie could see, she was a beauty. They sat close, she and Antonio, leaning toward each other with an intimacy and urgency that wrenched Cassie's heart. He held the girl's hand so firmly his knuckles shone white in the lamplight.

Cassie watched, stunned. Antonio was speaking earnestly to the woman, whispering endearments perhaps, so caught up in their conversation he had eyes for no one else in the room. The woman sat impassively watching him, listening, or perhaps not listening. Her mouth was turned down and she seemed unwilling to be convinced by his persuasive manner or eloquent words.

Cassie had seen enough. With a sour taste rising in her throat, she pivoted and strode out of the restaurant without looking back. As the door clattered behind her, she heard the hostess call out, "Miss, I can seat you now. Miss?"

Cassie climbed into her automobile and drove home, tears blinding her eyes. Why hadn't she seen it? Antonio was just like Drake...handsome, smooth talking, virile...and a womanizing fraud!

She cried herself to sleep that night, something she hadn't done in four long years. Why was God allowing her to repeat the same tragic mistake she had made with Drake? How could Antonio have shared such a special evening with her, and a few days later be involved with someone else?

When Cassie awoke the next morning, she thought at first she had dreamed the incident at the Grille.

Surely she hadn't seen Antonio there with another woman. Now, in the cold light of day, she reasoned there had to be some logical explanation. After all, it wasn't as if Antonio had pledged her his undying love. He was still free to see others, just as she was. Just because he was spending time with another woman didn't mean he didn't care about Cassie. Maybe he was there at the Grille breaking off the relationship so that he could devote himself to Cassie. Her mind raced with endless possibilities, anything to justify Antonio's behavior.

When he telephoned later that morning, she waited expectantly for him to bring up the subject and explain it away— Oh, by the way, I ran into an old friend last night...or, I broke it off with an old girlfriend last night because it's you I love, Cassandra— but he didn't mention their broken date, except to say, "I'm sorry about last night. I hope we can reschedule our dinner date at the Pacific Grille."

"Sure, I'd like that," she said without enthusiasm.

"What I really called about," said Antonio, "is arranging a final rehearsal time, to make sure we're ready for the crusade. It's coming up in a few days, you know."

"I know. We'll be performing twice the first night."

"I have a class tonight. Are you free to practice tomorrow evening?"

"Yes, but there's a children's program at the church. We won't be able to rehearse there."

"Then how about your house, Cass?"

"Not a good idea, if you want peace and quiet.

My sister Bree is bringing home one of her clients for a couple of days until there's space available at the shelter. A woman with a baby and a toddler." Cassie paused, an idea brewing. "What about your house, Antonio? Couldn't we practice there?" And maybe in the privacy of his own home he would open up to her.

"My house?" He sounded surprised, guarded.

"Yes. I've heard it's a beautiful place. I'd love to see it. And you said you have a fantastic grand piano."

There was a long pause before he replied, "All right. My house it is. Do you need directions?"

"No. My father was there the other day. He'll tell me how to get there. Shall we say seven o'clock?"

"Seven, it is."

Cassie hung up the receiver with a nagging weight in her chest. Antonio was obviously not eager to have her come to his home. Why? Was he keeping even more from her than she suspected? The old accusations others had made about Antonio came flooding back, along with a few of her own: He's a loner, aloof, reclusive. Never invites anyone to that big, fancy house of his. Makes you wonder what kind of man he is, and what secrets he's hiding.

The next evening, Cassie had mixed feelings as she drove to Antonio's home in Del Mar. She was curious to see his estate, but she hated the idea that she could no longer trust him. And she felt a splinter of guilt for manipulating an invitation to his house just to allay her suspicions.

As her automobile scaled the craggy bluff on

which was perched the imposing Pagliarulo mansion, she noticed a heavy fog rolling in off the ocean, bathing the regal house in a misty shroud. It was at once stunning and foreboding, like a scene out of an Edgar Alan Poe tale...a stately house with an ethereal, otherworldly quality. For one bizarre moment, she wondered, Is this house real and substantial or is it an eerie illusion, a mirage, as mysterious and inscrutable as the man who lives here?

As she parked her car and stepped out with her sheet music under her arm, she chided herself for letting her imagination run wild. This was just a house and Antonio was just a man, even if they both struck her as grandly imposing and larger than life.

With the fog coming in, I'd better make an early evening of it, she noted as she stepped between the two stone lions and treaded gingerly up the wide brick walkway. She rang the bell just once before the double doors opened and Antonio appeared, looking ruggedly handsome in a blue sport shirt and jeans.

"Right on time, Cassandra," he said as he ushered her inside.

She tried not to gape as she gazed around at the palatial surroundings—high-ceilinged rooms with crystal chandeliers, plush white carpets, and floor-to-ceiling windows that overlooked the ocean. "Your home...it's breathtaking." She had expected luxury, but this was opulence.

"God has blessed us," Antonio said quietly as he led her to the music room, a spacious room with a grand piano in the center and plush sofas and chairs surrounding it.

She brushed her fingertips over the piano's gleaming black surface. "You could have a miniconcert in this room."

He chuckled. "I suppose I could."

She wanted to ask him why he didn't open his magnificent house to friends and colleagues for parties and concerts and special gatherings. Why did he keep such beauty hidden from the rest of the world? But she couldn't bring herself to say the words. Was she afraid of the answer? Afraid of his reaction?

"Are you ready?" he asked, sitting down at the piano and moving his fingers lightly over the keys, playing the familiar strains of a praise song.

She sat down on the bench beside him. "I didn't realize you played."

"I don't. Only on my own piano, and for my own amusement."

"You play very well."

He reached over and clasped her hand. "No, Cassandra, you are the one who plays very well."

They had just run through one song when Juliana came breezing in with a tray of milk and fancy cookies. She set the tray on a nearby end table. "I don't mean to interrupt you two. You sound so wonderful together, but I thought you could use some nourishment. Cassandra, if you prefer coffee or tea or a soft drink…"

"No, milk is fine, especially with cookies. These look delicious."

"I wish I could say I baked them with my own two little hands, but I must confess. They're from the bakery."

Antonio scooped up several cookies and handed one to Cassie. "My mother has plied me with cookies and milk since I was a little boy...and she's still doing it."

"I think that's wonderful," Cassie said, nibbling the small shortbread delicacy.

"So do I," he agreed. "I hope she never changes."

Juliana slipped over beside the piano and gave Antonio a kiss on the cheek. "Well, son, I'll leave you two alone so you can finish your practice."

He patted her cheek. "You can stay and listen, if you wish."

"Oh, don't worry. I'll be listening from the other room."

They rehearsed for over an hour, then took a break for more cookies and milk. After another half hour of practice, Antonio heaved a contented sigh. "Well, if you ask me, that's as good as it gets. What do you say, Cassandra?"

She nodded. "I suppose I'm prejudiced, but I think we sound terrific. We're more than ready for the crusade."

"My sentiments exactly." He reached over and massaged her shoulder. "Are you running on adrenaline the way I am?"

"I'm tired, but yes, I feel like a clock wound too tight." She glanced at her watch. "Oh, my, it's later than I thought. I wanted to go before the fog rolled in."

"The fog...you're right. I suppose you'd better be going." He gathered her sheet music and walked with her out to the foyer. She felt a keen disappointment as he opened the door. She had come here tonight hoping for answers, for reassurance, and she had gotten neither. She had become so absorbed in their music, she had nearly forgotten Antonio's lie, his betrayal. Now it was time to leave and his behavior was still a mystery to her.

As they stepped onto the porch, he touched her arm. "Cassandra, you can't go."

She stared up at him, bewildered. "I can't?"

"No. Look. The fog is as thick as pea soup."

"But I must go. It's not a long drive. I'll go slow."

"You'll do no such thing. You'll stay here until the fog lifts. I won't have you risking your life."

"But it could linger all night."

"Then…then you'll stay here. My mother can make up a bed for you in one of the guest rooms." He paused, studying her intently. "You don't mind staying here, do you? It's entirely proper. My mother is here. She makes a very competent chaperon."

"Of course I don't mind." Cassie allowed him to lead her back inside. "I'd better phone my father. He'll be worried."

Antonio showed her to the phone. "You call your father. I'll have my mother prepare your room. Then you can drive home first thing in the morning. After breakfast, of course."

After Cassie phoned home, Antonio escorted her to the family room, where pine walls and a floor-to-ceiling stone fireplace gave the room a rustic air. He turned on the wide-screen television and slipped a videotape into the VCR. "I'm taking a chance you're fond of old black-and-white films. Henry Fonda...Humphrey Bogart...Audrey Hepburn..."

Cassie sat down on the white leather sofa. "Gary Cooper...Barbara Stanwyck...Clark Gable... I love them all."

"Terrific. So, unless you're too tired, I thought we'd relax a little and watch a vintage flick before turning in."

She smiled. "Sounds good to me." Maybe now, in the solitude of his own home, Antonio would confide in her about the mysterious woman he seemed so enamored with at the Pacific Grille.

Antonio picked up the remote control and sat down beside Cassie. He clicked on the movie, adjusted the sound, and settled back, draping his arm around the back of the sofa, not quite touching her shoulder. But his closeness was enough to stir her emotions. How she yearned for him to gather her into his arms and kiss her the way he had that night at the Pacific Grille. But what if that kiss had meant nothing to him? He had already gone back to the restaurant with another woman. Maybe he took a different woman every week. Cassie had no way of knowing how fickle he might be, or whether he considered her anything more than a friend.

She gazed up at him, studying the way the flickering screen cast dancing lights and shadows over his stalwart face. He was the most attractive man she had ever known, and she was on the verge of falling in love with him. But what chance was there he felt the same way about her?

He caught her gaze and smiled, his dusky eyes crinkling in that way that sent a tickle through her stomach. "You're supposed to be watching the movie," he murmured.

"I am," she said, blushing slightly.

"Really? So am I." He moved closer, his arm slipping around her shoulders. Searching her eyes, he traced the line of her chin with his fingertips. "But who needs TV, when the view is so much better right here?"

"I thought so, too," she whispered, mesmerized by those eyes.

Ever so slowly he lowered his head to hers and kissed her gently, his lips moving over hers with extraordinary tenderness. His sweet, musky warmth and nearness sent a delicious dizziness spiraling through her. Her heart sang. He felt the same irresistible attraction to her that she felt for him. Maybe they were meant to be together after all.

After several heady, intoxicating moments, Antonio broke away and released her. "It's late," he said, his voice husky. He looked shaken, unnerved.

She smoothed back her tousled curls, keenly disappointed. "I—I hadn't noticed."

He stood up and arched his broad shoulders. "I'd better let you get your beauty sleep, Cassandra."

She stood and faced him, the television sounds playing in the background. A love scene with violins and a soprano saxophone, but the music could have been playing for her and Antonio. He clasped both of her hands in his. "Come. I'll show you to your room."

She held her ground. "Wait, Antonio."

He gazed down quizzically at her. "What is it?"

"That's what I want to know." She forced out the words. She had to know. "What just happened here? The kiss. What does it mean?"

His brow furrowed. His fingers tightened around hers. "It means I care about you, Cassandra."

Her hopes soared. "Care about me?"

"More than you can imagine."

"I care about you, too, Antonio. But I need to know...where are we going with this?"

His jaw tightened and he released her hands. "I can't answer that."

"It's not like...I mean, I'm not asking for a commitment," she stammered, flustered, tongue-tied. "I—I just need to know what you're thinking...how you feel."

"I told you, Cassandra." His voice took on a sudden hard edge. He was closing up, pushing her away with his dark, smoldering expression, his eyes flashing fire. "I care about you more than I expected. More than I ever dreamed possible. But I'm not looking for a serious relationship. I can't."

"You can't? Why not?"

"It's out of the question. I've got...responsibilities, obligations you know nothing about."

"Can you tell me about them?" She was grasping at straws now, on the verge of desperation. She hated this feeling. It was the same crushing sensation she had experienced when she realized Drake could never be part of her life. "Please talk to me, Antonio. I'm a good listener."

"No, Cassandra. I'm sorry. I'm not free to tell you. Not now. Perhaps not ever. If it weren't for my own weakness, this infuriating, unrelenting need to be close to you..." His voice trailed off. He turned and strode across the room and snapped off the television. "It's late. I'll see you upstairs."

They climbed the wide, circular staircase in a desultory silence. She followed him to the end of the hall, where he opened a door and snapped on a light, then stepped back so she could enter. "This is the only guest room with its own balcony, sitting room and bath. And I'm sure my mother laid out a fresh nightgown and robe for you. You should be quite comfortable."

"I'm sure I will be," she said quietly. "Thank you, Antonio."

He leaned down and brushed a chaste kiss on her cheek. "Good night, Cassandra. Sweet dreams."

But there was no way Cassie would have sweet dreams tonight. Even after a warm bubble bath, she was too keyed up to sleep. She tossed and turned for nearly an hour in the queen-size canopy bed before drifting into a restless slumber punctuated by bizarre, disjointed dreams. In one nightmarish scenario, she found herself in a satin wedding gown walking down the aisle of a church on Antonio's arm. But when she reached the altar, she looked over and saw Drake standing beside her, a sinister smile on his lips as he said, "Looks like we'll be together forever after all, Cass." As he broke into raucous laughter, she covered her face and screamed.

The sound woke her and she sat up in bed, trembling, not sure whether she herself had screamed or whether it was someone else, or no one. Since the house remained dark and silent, the scream must have come from her own overactive imagination.

Cassie lay back down and tucked the downy comforter around her, then fluffed her pillow and rolled over, one way, then the other. But no matter how much she tossed and turned, sleep eluded her. She stared up at the ceiling and listened to a branch tapping against a windowpane with a scratchy rat-a-tat. She thought about Antonio sleeping in another room in the house, so close to her, and yet so far. How ironic that the more she cared for him, the more distant he became. He was a mystery, a conundrum, always just out of reach, just beyond her understanding.

Sometime around 3:00 a.m., Cassie climbed out of bed and walked over to the sliding door and drew back the vertical blinds. Pale, opalescent moonlight streamed into the room. Amazingly, the fog had lifted and the sky was clear and studded with stars. Enormous waves were rolling in with their foamy whitecaps, their distant roar like an enchantment, a mother's soothing murmur, a baby's cradle song.

Cassie shivered and hugged herself. She felt very small suddenly, like a lonely child in need of her mother's comforting arms. But Cassie's mother was dead, and no matter how much Cassie yearned for her arms, she would never feel them around her again, at least not on this side of heaven. Thinking of her mother made her feel even more alone and isolated. The shadowed room suddenly felt stuffy, too warm, suffocating.

Cassie pulled on her silk robe, opened the sliding door and stepped out onto the balcony. For early November, the weather was surprisingly warm, the night wind brisk but balmy. Cassie walked to the railing and stared down at the shimmering sea. She inhaled sharply, clearing her head of cobwebs and those wild, unsettling dreams. She was feeling better. Maybe she could sleep now.

But as her gaze moved randomly over the moonlit beach below, she spotted something that started her blood pumping. Two figures on the beach...a strapping man in sport shirt and jeans carrying a delicate woman in a filmy white gown, her ebony hair streaming behind her. From the tender way he carried her nestled against his chest, they were obviously very much in love.

But Cassie's blood turned cold as she recognized the couple.

It was Antonio and the young woman from the Pacific Grille!

Chapter Eleven

From her balcony, Cassie stared incredulously at the couple on the beach below. It couldn't be Antonio…but, undeniably, it was. There was no mistaking that physique, that face, that walk. A shard of disappointment tore at Cassie's heart. How could it be? Her Antonio…the man who had kissed her so tenderly just hours ago…out on a moonlit stroll with another woman, someone he obviously knew intimately.

Cassie wrapped her flimsy robe around her and slipped back inside the darkened bedroom. Quietly she shut the sliding door and made her way back to the canopy bed. Like a soldier wounded in battle, she crawled between the covers and curled in a fetal position, hugging her knees against her chest. She pressed her fist against her mouth to keep from sobbing.

After a while she heard the front door open downstairs. She listened carefully. Yes. Footsteps on the stairs, an occasional step creaking. Cassie slipped out of bed and opened her door a crack. At the opposite end of the hall, shafts of moonlight streaming through the skylight revealed the silhouette of a man and a woman. Antonio, still carrying the delicate woman in his arms, opened a door and disappeared inside.

Cassie shut her own door and returned to bed. She lay still, staring up into the darkness, her heart still pounding fiercely. What had she just seen? And what did it mean?

The answer was evident. The woman in Antonio's arms lived in this very house. She wasn't just a girlfriend or a passing flirtation. She was Antonio's wife. His wife!

But why, in the name of heaven, did he keep her a secret? What terrible thing has happened that he felt it necessary to hide her from his friends and colleagues and the world at large?

Cassie's thoughts raced. Maybe she's an invalid and can't walk. Or she's suffering from some debilitating or degenerative disease. Maybe she can't be a real wife to him, but he's too loyal to leave her. Maybe she's lost her mind. But no, she didn't seem insane. But she could be emotionally troubled.

Cassie recalled the day she spotted them at the restaurant. The woman had looked forlorn, withdrawn, despondent, while Antonio appeared to be trying fervently to reason with her. What issues divided them? What conflicts spurred Antonio to seek solace in the arms of another woman?

Cassie winced. She was that other woman. But whatever struggles Antonio and his wife were experiencing, he had no right to keep his marriage a secret. He had no right to court Cassie and lead her to believe he cared for her when he was already committed to another.

Antonio's words earlier this evening came crashing back into Cassie's mind, taking on an ominous new meaning: *I've got responsibilities, obligations you know nothing about.*

"You sure do!" Cassie said brokenly. "The most profound obligation of all…a wife! How could you do this to me, Antonio? Or to her? To yourself! I thought you were a decent, honorable man. A godly man."

Cassie threw back her covers and climbed out of bed. She turned on a light and reached for her clothes. It was only 4:00 a.m., but she had had enough. She was going home. "I was wrong before, and I'm wrong again," she muttered as she pulled on her blouse and slacks. "First, Drake and now Antonio. But, God help me, I'll never let myself be deceived by a man again!"

She slipped into her shoes, grabbed her purse and sheet music and stole quietly out of her room, down the stairs, and out the door. She prayed Antonio wouldn't hear her car starting and come running out. But after being up half the night on the beach with his wife, he was probably sleeping soundly beside her now and dreaming with the angels.

When Cassie arrived home, she quietly let herself in and stole upstairs on tiptoe. She didn't want her father or sisters waking and wondering why she was coming home in the middle of the night. It would be hard enough in the morning to admit the truth about Antonio.

In her room, she undressed and collapsed into bed and pulled her pillow over her head, as if that might shut out the pain of Antonio's betrayal. She fell into a troubled sleep, but all too soon it was morning, with sunlight pouring through the window and the sounds of a busy household stirring downstairs. Cassie considered spending the day in bed brooding, but she wasn't about to cave in emotionally over Antonio the way she had over Drake. If she had learned one thing from Drake, it was that she could survive a broken romance. After all, she had survived the greatest heartache…losing her beloved mother. Somehow she would put her feelings for Antonio out of her mind. But that wouldn't be easy when she was scheduled to perform with him at the crusade in a few days.

Cassie showered and dressed and ran a brush through her hair, then steeled herself emotionally and trudged downstairs. She knew already that her father and sisters would besiege her with questions. After all, no matter how innocent and proper it might have been, she had spent the night at Antonio's palatial estate. They would want to know every detail.

Sure enough, the moment she took her place at the breakfast table, Bree and Frannie started plying her with questions. "What is his house like?… What did you do?… Was he romantic?"

Cassie poured herself a cup of coffee and kept her

gaze lowered. "The house is gorgeous. A real mansion. With a breathtaking view of the ocean. And that's all I'm saying on the subject."

"But what about Antonio?" pressed Frannie, sounding disappointed. "Did the two of you get closer? Do you think he's getting serious?"

"How do you feel about him?" asked Bree. "You do like him a lot, don't you?"

Cassie inhaled deeply and sipped her coffee, even though it was too hot and nearly scalded her throat. "I have nothing more to say right now," she said, her tone clipped. She felt her lower lip quiver, so she took another sip of coffee.

Frannie crossed her arms in displeasure. "That's no fair. We tell you everything."

"Everything?" quizzed their father with a twinkle in his eyes.

"Maybe not everything," Frannie conceded, "but almost!"

"Well, I have a feeling Cassie will tell us what we need to know when the time is right. Right, muffin?"

"Right, Daddy." She was on the verge of tears already. She met her father's gaze and knew he sensed something was wrong, but he was wise enough not to push for answers. That was her darling daddy, always knowing the right thing to say...or not to say.

"Well, if we're not getting an earful," Frannie said, pushing back her chair, "I'm going to the sunroom to work on my sculpture."

"And I'd better get over to the shelter and see how my client is doing," Bree stated.

Cassie looked around curiously. "That's right. You were bringing a woman and her children home for a few days. What happened?"

"I was able to get them into a shelter at the last minute."

"Oh, that's good." Cassie wasn't sure she could have handled a baby crying and a toddler running around the house this morning.

Brianna came around the table and put a hand on Cassie's shoulder. "Are you okay, Cass? You look like...like you had a hard night."

Cassie steadied her voice. She refused to break down in front of her sister. "I did. I'll tell you about it later."

"Sure thing." Bree leaned over the chair and gave her an impromptu hug. "I'll keep you in my prayers today, even if I don't know what I'm praying for."

Cassie managed a forced, lopsided grin. "Good. I can use all the prayers I can get."

After her sisters had left the room, Cassie looked up at her father and let him see her misery. Tears swam in her eyes and spilled onto her cheeks. "Oh, Daddy!" she moaned.

He got out of his chair, came over and took her by the hand. "Come on, baby girl. Let's go to my study."

They walked down the hall to the comfortable, paneled room her father called his study, and he shut the door behind them. She curled up in the old leather chair across from his rolltop desk, her favorite chair since she was a little girl. She used to sit here and watch him working on his sermons, and he'd slip her hard candy from his desk drawer.

"Do you feel like talking, Cass?" he asked, settling down in the nubby, overstuffed chair beside her.

"No," she said, sniffing, "but I've got to tell someone."

Haltingly she told him the whole story about seeing Antonio with the woman at the restaurant and then last night on the beach. "She lives there in his house, Daddy. I saw him carry her upstairs to their room and go inside. She's his wife! He has a wife, Daddy, and he never said a word about her."

Her father sat forward and rubbed his jaw, deep in thought. "He told you he's married?"

"No! He doesn't even know I know about her! But isn't it obvious? She's living there at his house. She's not some casual friend. The way he carried her on the beach, with such tender care, I could see how much he loves her."

Her father's brow furrowed. "This might explain something strange that happened a few days ago when I visited Juliana. There was a crash upstairs and I heard a woman scream."

Cassie sat at attention. "It must have been her."

"I asked Juliana about it, but she virtually shooed me out of the house. I could tell she was upset and concerned, but she wouldn't give me a clue what was going on."

Cassie put her fingers to her lips, her voice hushed. "Oh, Daddy, I didn't think about it until now, but

Juliana is obviously keeping Antonio's secret. That means *she's* deceived us, too.''

"It looks that way, honey." He heaved a disgruntled sigh. "There's only one way to handle this."

"How?"

"We get on the phone and tell Antonio and Juliana we want to talk to them. We get this out in the open and find out what's going on."

Cassie shook her head. "No, Daddy, I can't. I'm too humiliated. I don't want to ever see Antonio again."

"That's going to be hard to manage. The two of you are performing together in a few days. Besides, maybe Antonio has a reasonable explanation. I pegged him as a decent, honorable man. And Juliana...she's as open and forthright as any woman I've ever met. I can't believe the two of them would deliberately deceive us."

Cassie saw something in her father's eyes that startled her—a wounded, deeply disappointed expression. "This is hurting you, too, isn't it, Daddy? You care a lot about Juliana."

Thoughtfully he massaged his temples. "I am very fond of her. We've become good friends. I would hate to think I can't trust her."

Cassie asked the question that played in her mind. "Are you falling for her, Daddy?"

He met her gaze with a grimace. "I don't know, honey. Maybe I care more than I thought. Or maybe it's just that I always figured I was a good judge of character. It's hard for me to believe I struck out twice, with both Antonio and his mother."

Cassie reached over and patted her father's hand. "And to think I wanted to get you and Juliana together. I really thought she would make you happy."

He locked fingers with her and flashed an ironic smile. "Truth is, Cass, in my mind I practically had you and Antonio walking down the aisle. I thought he was exactly the kind of man you needed. I'm afraid my matchmaking skills are no better than yours."

"We're quite a pair," she lamented.

"I promise. No more matchmaking. I've learned my lesson."

"Me, too, Daddy." They were both silent for several moments. Finally Cassie asked, "How am I going to perform with him in the crusade, knowing what I know?"

The lines around her father's mouth tightened. "That's why you should confront him, Cass. If he's being unfaithful to his wife, even emotionally unfaithful, I don't want him taking part in the crusade...."

"But what if I'm mistaken, Daddy? What if I read the signals wrong? What if he thinks we're just good friends, and that's all there is to it?"

"That's why you've got to talk to him, Cass. Get things out in the open. Clear the air. Know where you stand."

"I want to, Daddy, but I just can't face him with my suspicions before the crusade. Afterward I will. Then our performances will be over, and I'll never have to see him again."

Her father eyed her intently. "You really want to go ahead and perform with him?"

"Yes, I do. What if he's had a valid reason for the way he's behaved? If his wife is ill, it must be very painful for him. And it's not like he's made any promises to me. I just believed what I wanted to believe. He even told me he had obligations I knew nothing about. So I think he's been trying to tell me his secret all along."

"Well, we'll give Antonio a few days and see how well he imparts his secret. If he hasn't told you the truth by the end of the crusade, I'm confronting the man myself."

Cassie stood up and kissed her father on the top of his head. "Thanks for listening, Daddy. Pray for me, okay?"

"I always do, baby girl."

Cassie slipped out of the study and made her way to the music room. A couple of hours of invigorating practice would help restore her spirits. But just as she sat down, the phone rang. She grabbed it up, thinking of Antonio. But it was another man's voice. "Cassie? That you?"

"Yes. Is that you, Drake?"

"Well, things are improving. You recognized my voice."

"What do you want, Drake?"

"Like I said the other day, I want to see you, Cassie. We have a lot to catch up on. I know I made a lot of mistakes in the past, but I'm not the man you remember."

"Then who are you?" she asked dryly.

"That's what I like to see...healthy curiosity. I'm a man who has faced a lot of difficulties, Cass, and I've come through stronger and wiser. Give me a chance to show you the new me. Go out with me just once, and if you don't like what you see, I'll leave town and never bother you again."

"Is that a promise?"

"You bet."

Cassie had an idea. "All right, I'll see you, Drake, but on my own terms."

"Whatever you say, Cass."

"Come to my father's crusade at our church."

"His crusade? Listen, Cass, you know me. I'm not a very religious man."

"I'm not asking you to be religious. I'm asking you to come and hear what my father has to say, that's all."

Drake sighed deeply. "Okay, I'm game, as long as we spend some time together afterward."

"That's not part of the deal," she countered.

Drake slipped into his most persuasive voice. "Come on, Cass. Just a little dinner together after the show, er, I mean, crusade. What can it hurt?"

Cassie weighed the possibilities. Was she foolish to associate with Drake again so soon after being hurt by Antonio? But she needed something...someone...to help her forget. Why not Drake? He was unattached now. She ignored the niggling little voice that said, *Not according to God's law!*

"I'll go to dinner with you after the crusade," she said at last, "but just as friends. Is that understood?"

"Crystal clear, Cass. Give me the pertinent information about the crusade, and I'll be there with bells on."

She smiled in spite of herself. "Bells aren't necessary. Just come with an open mind and heart that God can fill."

Chapter Twelve

That evening, after his troubling conversation with Cassie, Andrew decided to spend some time alone in his bedroom retreat. He settled into his favorite creaky rocker and gazed out at the moonlit sky. How he wished he had Mandy here to confide in. She always had a way of lifting his spirits and making him see things in a positive light. But what would she say if she knew he and Cassie were being deceived by two people they were just beginning to love and trust?

"Mandy, my precious Mandy," he said aloud, his voice hardly more than a whisper, "I'm a weaker man than I thought. When Cassie told me about Antonio and Juliana, I wanted to be strong for her. Wanted to say the right thing. Be comforting and consoling. But the truth is, I was shaken. I kept thinking about Juliana. How my feelings were already tied up in knots over her. How could I comfort my daughter when my own heart was wounded?"

Andrew sat forward and raked his fingers through his thick hair. "I'm a stupid man, Mandy. After five years of being faithful to your memory, I let myself fall for this woman. Juliana Pagliarulo. And now I'm angry with myself for being so blind. Okay, Mandy, I admit it. My pride is hurt. I thought this woman respected me, cared about me. Then how could she look me in the eye, smile sweetly, and lie to me?"

Did she really lie? Or have you simply not given her the opportunity to tell you the truth? The thought struck Andrew like a slap. Maybe Juliana wanted to tell him the truth about her son, but hadn't known how. Maybe she was afraid. Or maybe Antonio had forbidden her to say a word. Or maybe she was just waiting for the right moment. Andrew owed her a chance to come clean. Maybe if he prompted her a little, she would spill out the whole story, and her candor would restore his trust in her. It was a long shot, but he had to try.

Before he lost his nerve, he went to the phone on the night stand and dialed her number. Thank goodness, she answered, and not Antonio. She responded positively when he suggested they have lunch together tomorrow, but when he suggested he pick her up at her home, she promptly replied, "Oh, Andrew, that's not necessary. I'll meet you at the restaurant."

She doesn't want you running into Antonio's wife! came a silent accusation. He hung up the receiver feeling more troubled than he had before he phoned her. More and more, it looked like Juliana was playing him for a fool, the same way Antonio was hoodwinking Cassie.

Andrew met Juliana at noon the next day at a coffee shop halfway between their homes. He had deliberately chosen a modest, lackluster restaurant that offered no illusion of romance. After all, his purpose today wasn't courtship or even friendship; he was on a fact-finding mission.

Juliana greeted him with the same charm and savoir faire she always exhibited. She looked stunning in a red velvet dress that enhanced her hourglass figure. For a moment Andrew wanted to disregard his suspicions and simply enjoy Juliana's captivating beauty. But he had to keep a clear head if he was going to grill her without breaking his promise to Cassie to keep silent about their suspicions.

After he had ordered the steak lunch and she a caesar salad, they gazed at each other across the table. "What is it, Andrew?" she asked lightly. "You look so serious today."

He drummed his fingers on the shiny tabletop. "I just have a lot on my mind lately."

She smiled invitingly. "I'm a good listener."

He smiled faintly. "I'm counting on that, Juliana."

"So tell me," she urged. "What makes you look so solemn?"

"The truth is, I've been thinking a lot about my daughter and your son."

Juliana nodded, her smile lingering. "What a coincidence, Andrew. So have I."

"And what conclusions have you reached?"

Her dark eyes danced. "I know my son cares

deeply for Cassandra. I think they make a wonderful couple. Don't you?''

He sat back and inhaled deeply. ''Yes, I thought so, too. But my opinion isn't at issue here. What I want to know is your opinion, Juliana. Tell me honestly what you think. Do you see a future for them?''

''Possibly.'' She traced a scroll design on the table with one long lacquered nail. ''I think they could be very happy together.''

''Yes, that thought crossed my mind, as well.''

''You...you sound as if you have doubts.''

Andrew sat forward and searched Juliana's eyes. ''Tell me one thing. Is there anything you know that would keep the two of them apart? Any reason they should not be together?''

Juliana lowered her gaze, a slight frown creasing her brow.

''There is something, isn't there?'' challenged Andrew, his own emotions roiling. ''A reason they can never marry?''

Juliana was silent for a long moment.

''Please, Juliana, my daughter's future is at stake. Be honest with me.''

Juliana's frown gave way to an alluring smile. She tossed her head jauntily, her ebony hair rippling over her shoulders. ''Of course I am honest with you, Andrew. I would love to see our children marry someday. Antonio deserves some happiness, and your daughter has made my son happier than he has been in many years.''

''Then, as far as you're concerned, there's nothing

standing in their way? No reason they can't be married?''

Juliana drew her words carefully. ''Nothing that can't be worked out. And I will do everything in my power to help him.''

''Then there is something? Some problem?'' pressed Andrew.

Again, Juliana seemed cautious with her reply. ''Not in my estimation. In my mind, Antonio acts out of misguided loyalty, out of guilt. He takes on burdens he shouldn't have to bear.''

''Guilt? Burdens?'' repeated Andrew, his hackles rising.

''Duties. Responsibilities.'' Juliana waved her hand, looking flustered. ''I tell him it is time for him to be free, but he will not listen to me. He feels he must keep his promise…he must sacrifice himself for—'' Juliana covered her mouth and shook her head. ''Oh, I am saying too much.''

Tension danced along Andrew's spine. His heart raced. Did this woman have the gall to suggest her son leave his bedridden wife for another woman…for Andrew's daughter? He clenched his fists to keep his agitation under control. ''No, Juliana, you're not saying nearly enough,'' he said sharply. ''For what…or whom…does Antonio feel he must sacrifice himself?''

Juliana's discomposure turned to a grimace of suspicion. ''Why are you asking me these questions, Andrew?''

''No reason, really.'' Now he was the one tweaking the truth.

"You seem so different today. So morose. So solemn. Not your usual jolly self." She gave him a teasing smile. "I miss the old Andrew. Where has he gone?"

"Nowhere. I'm the same old feisty, fun-loving chap I've always been," he said thickly. "But, frankly, I am concerned."

"About your daughter?"

"And your son."

Juliana laughed lightly. "Oh, Andrew, you worry too much. They are not children. They are old enough to know what they want. Yes, they may have troubles to overcome, but they will be fine!"

"I'm not so sure about that, Juliana."

Her smile faded. "You are worried, aren't you? Why, Andrew? Has someone been talking to you?"

"Now who's jumping to conclusions?" he said evasively.

"I see it in your eyes, Andrew. The anger, the distress. Tell me, what is it? Are there rumors?"

"Rumors?"

"Please, Andrew, what have you heard?"

"Nothing." He drew back, suddenly on the defensive, his heart pounding. "Nothing to speak of."

"But you have heard something?"

Perspiration beaded on his forehead. "Yes."

She sat forward, her hands clasped tightly. "Tell me."

He groped for the right words, but there were none. He wanted to have it out with her, but he couldn't. He had promised Cassie. "I'm sorry, Juliana. I shouldn't have gotten into this."

"Sorry? Sorry about what? What are you talking about?"

He shifted in his chair. Why had he thought he could broach this subject without breaking a confidence? "Listen, let's just drop it, okay?" He looked around for their waitress. "Our food should be here any time."

Juliana's gaze remained riveted on him. "Don't wriggle out of this, Andrew. Say what you mean. Tell me what you've heard."

Now he was in the hot seat. He wiped his forehead with his handkerchief. "I can't, Juliana. I've already spoken out of turn."

"This thing...it is about Antonio? Something bad about Antonio?"

"I'm sorry," he said miserably. "I'm not free to say."

Juliana straightened her shoulders, her eyes blazing. "Andrew, what is this about? You invited me for a pleasant lunch, and here we are together, and now, now everything has changed, and you are closed up as a little mouse. You are angry, but you will not even tell me why. How can we have a happy time together if you do not tell me what's wrong?"

Andrew shook his head. Man, this had backfired big time. "I told you, Juliana—"

She finished for him. "I know, Andrew, I know. You are not free to say." Her usually musical voice rose a decibel. "Well, neither am I!"

His misery was growing. "Please understand, Juliana. I made a promise."

"So did I, Andrew! And, like you, I keep my

promises." She reached for her handbag. "Apparently we have said everything and nothing in this conversation, and now we have nothing more to say to each other, so I will excuse myself and go home."

He reached out and clasped her hand. "Don't go. Please! We haven't even eaten yet."

She stood, extricated her hand from his, and smoothed her red skirt. "Obviously this wasn't a lunch date, Andrew," she said hotly. "It was a fishing expedition."

Andrew jumped to his feet and stared Juliana down. "That's not what I intended, Juliana. I'm just concerned about our children, and I'm convinced you have the answers."

"I have no answers. Even if I did, do you think my son would listen to me? He has a mind of his own. He does what he wishes."

"And what is it he wishes, Juliana? To marry my daughter in spite of his 'obligations'? Is that it?"

"I cannot speak for my son, Andrew. He speaks for himself!" She squared her shoulders and tucked her purse under her arm. "And now that I have lost my appetite, I will go."

Andrew touched her arm. "Wait, Juliana. If your son has nothing to hide, why are you acting so guilty? Why are you running away?"

A sad, pleading look flickered in her dark eyes. "I'm sorry, Andrew. Some things are not mine to tell."

Before he could reply, she pivoted and strode briskly out of the restaurant without a backward glance. He considered running after her, but what could he say? They would be at the same infuriating impasse, neither willing to betray a confidence.

Andrew paid for their uneaten lunches and as an afterthought told the waitress to bag up the food and he would take it home. He was a frugal man at heart and the steak and salad would make a satisfying midnight repast. And as disturbed and frustrated as he was feeling right now, he would probably be up well past midnight.

Late that evening, after his daughters had gone to bed, Andrew climbed the stairs to his bedroom retreat. He hadn't bothered with the midnight snack; in fact, he hadn't been hungry all day. All he could think about was his disastrous lunch date with Juliana and the terrible rift between them now. How he had hoped she would be open and forthright with him. Instead, out of misplaced loyalty, she was keeping her son's loathsome secret, at Cassie's expense!

What sort of woman was she?

A woman Andrew was falling in love with.

There! He had admitted it to himself. No matter how hard he tried to argue the feelings away, he was more than a little smitten with Juliana. And the fact that she had deceived him only made his heart ache all the more.

Andrew entered his darkened room and made his way through the shadows to his favorite rocker by the window. No sense in turning on a light. He knew this room like the back of his hand, and right now the darkness felt somehow comforting. He settled back in his chair and gazed out at the blackened sky, almost void of starlight. Where was the moon tonight, that trusty whitewashed globe he always depended on? Ah, yes, there it was. Hardly more than a fingernail tonight. About as fragile and dim as Andrew's own disheartened spirit.

"Lord, I've made a mess of things, haven't I? Acting like a smug, self-righteous jerk? Thinking I can right all wrongs? Man, what a pompous, overblown ego!"

Now he'd be lucky if Juliana didn't go home and tell Antonio the Rowlands family was on to him, and then Cassie would find out and have her father's head for betraying her confidence. But then the truth would be out and he and Cassie could get on with their lives without the likes of Antonio and Juliana.

There was just one hitch. Andrew didn't want to give up on Juliana. No matter what she had done, he cared for her, yearned for her in a way he hadn't felt in years. That part of his life had been dead for so long, he had nearly forgotten how much a man could want a woman. Of course, it wasn't the same way he had loved Mandy; it was a different kind of love, but just as valid and powerful. And now, just when he had begun to love someone again, he was already losing her.

Andrew reached for his Bible and held it unopened on his lap. Just running his palm over its worn leather binding made him feel God was closer. Andrew needed that now, God's comforting presence, His Spirit whispering consolation in his battle-weary heart.

The citywide crusade was just two days away, and Andrew didn't feel ready. How could he get up in the pulpit and preach night after night to hundreds of people when his own spirit felt dry and thirsty? The very real possibility that two people he cared for were deceiving him and wounding his daughter left him feeling demoralized, heartsick.

"Lord, I need You," he said aloud, his voice filling the stillness. "I've gotten my eyes off You today and I'm slipping. I'm like that old feisty fisherman Peter, Your impetuous, headstrong disciple, who insisted on walking on water, and he was fine as long as he kept his eyes on You. But the minute he looked at the raging waves around him, he was a goner. Down he plunged into the briny deep. That's me, Lord. I'm sinking fast, under a wave of circumstances I never expected, and I'm in a tailspin. Get me back on sure footing, Father, with my eyes focused only on You, so I can do the job You gave me to do."

Andrew lapsed into silence, waiting on God, listening with his heart. He had always had a knack for doing all the talking and trying to force his personal agenda on God, but he had learned over the years to simply sit quietly and listen to the soundless stirrings of the Almighty.

He had learned something else over the years. He knew what it was like for a mere mortal to commune with God. And he knew how easy it was to miss that blessing. Out of a sense of duty he could read his Bible and even pray and still not connect with the Lord, still not feel the sweet presence of His Spirit moving in his soul, communing with him.

Only when Andrew stopped everything—the wild

rushing of his thoughts, his impatient awareness of time, his rising anxieties over the problems of the day…only then, when he made himself sit in silence and, like Peter, focus on the person of Jesus instead of his circumstances…only then did he feel God filling up the emptiness inside him. And as he released his anxieties, he was free to express his love and offer praises to his Savior. And soon the floodgates opened and poured God's love back on him…until the moment became transcendent. He and God in sweet communion. There was nothing on earth to match that glorious kinship. It was what God had planned for His children from the beginning.

But tonight Andrew felt far removed from the spiritual camaraderie he usually shared with his Heavenly Father. He had allowed the cares of the world to rob him of his joy; one "care" in particular named Juliana Pagliarulo. Putting his head in his hands, he said aloud in a voice broken with emotion, "Lord, it's going to be a long night, but I'm going to sit here and read Your Word and listen to Your Spirit until I've got my joy back and my eyes focused only on You."

Chapter Thirteen

On the first night of the crusade, Cassie was filled with a nervous excitement, a mixture of apprehension and anticipation as she watched the crowds stream into the sprawling auditorium, their voices blending like a discordant melody, pleasant, yet jarring, their words an indecipherable buzz. The choir was already in place onstage; her father and several pastors from other churches were sitting in a semicircle on the platform, and the minister of music was at the podium ready to lead the audience in an opening hymn.

Cassie sat beside Antonio off to one side near the grand piano. They would be performing after the congregational singing, doing a medley of traditional hymns with Cassie's own arrangements. She had looked forward to this evening for weeks, but now that it was here, she struggled with misgivings. She had asked God to let their performance be a blessing to others, but her heart was divided. She wanted to give the performance of her life, but her mind kept flashing back to the vision of Antonio with the mysterious woman on the beach. Since that night she had deliberately avoided Antonio, canceling their last practice session and assuring him they were more than ready for their performance.

Now she could avoid him no longer. They must perform together with a oneness and synergy she hardly felt. But God could give her His grace and strength, if she focused only on Him. That's what her father had reminded her this morning. Don't look at your circumstances; don't look at the mere mortals around you; look only to Him, and He will see you through.

She repeated those words in her mind minutes later when it was time to step up to the piano and accompany Antonio. As she placed her fingers on the ivory keys, she said inwardly, *This is for You, Lord. Let me be Your obedient child. You play through me.*

As her fingers danced over the keys and Antonio began to sing in his rich tenor, all other distractions slipped away. The grandeur of the songs and their message of hope gripped her emotions and made her heart soar. It was as if God Himself were taking pleasure in the fruit of the talent He had given her. The moment was inexpressible.

The blissful feeling lasted until the service was over. After several people from the congregation congratulated them on an outstanding performance, Antonio turned to her and flashed that beguiling smile of his. "They're right. You were wonderful, Cassandra." His voice flowed like honey as he took both her hands in his. "Performing with you was pure joy."

She mumbled an awkward reply while trying to disengage her hands from his, but he held her fast. "The night is young, Cassandra. Let's go out and celebrate. How about a midnight dinner for two at the Pacific Grille?"

"I—I can't," she stammered, scouring her mind for a credible excuse. The Pacific Grille was the last place she wanted to be. And with Antonio? Never!

"Of course you can go," he said, still beaming that bewitching smile at her. "Come now! Don't tell me you have another date."

"Actually, she does" came the deep-voiced reply behind her.

Whirling around, Cassie gazed up into the familiar, distinctive face of Drake Cameron. He stood there, tall, dark, attractive, with his usual natty, professorial air. His shiny black hair was slicked back from his high forehead and he had a twinkle in his crinkly, charcoal-gray eyes. She was momentarily speechless. Heaven help her, she had forgotten he was attending tonight's crusade. And she had promised to have dinner with him afterward.

At last she found her voice. "Drake, I—I wasn't sure you would come."

"And miss a chance to be with my favorite gal? Are you kidding? I've made reservations at the Blue Ox. If we hurry—"

Antonio broke in. "Mister, I think there must be some mistake. Cassandra and I have dinner plans."

Cassie looked up at Antonio and winced. How on

earth was she going to handle this diplomatically? "I'm sorry, Antonio," she said in a small, mortified voice, "but we don't have plans. I agreed to have dinner with Drake...Mr. Cameron...an old friend." With a nervous flutter of her hand, she said, "Drake, I'd like you to meet Antonio Pagliarulo. Antonio, this is Drake Cameron."

The two men shook hands stiffly while Antonio cast a wounded, sidelong glance at Cassie. "Yes, I've heard about you, Mr. Cameron."

"Well, I haven't heard nearly enough about you, Mr. Paglia..."

"Pagliarulo."

"Right. You have quite a voice. Very impressive," said Drake with a little chuckle. He turned and slipped his arm possessively around Cassie's waist. "Hate to break this up, but we're running late. Ready to go, sweetheart?"

Cassie gave Antonio a helpless, beseeching glance. He looked back at her with eyes full of hurt and disappointment.

"Then I guess I'll see you tomorrow night at the crusade, Antonio," she said, the words sounding thick on her tongue.

Antonio's gaze was withering. "Yes, Cassandra. Tomorrow night. You have a good evening." He turned to Drake. "A pleasure to meet you, Mr. Cameron."

"No, the pleasure's all mine," said Drake with a hefty grin.

As Cassie walked away on Drake's arm, she felt as if she were betraying Antonio. And yet why should she feel guilty when it was Antonio who had betrayed her with his seductive lies? Still, her heart was heavy with regret and misgivings.

Somehow Cassie managed to make it out of the church without collapsing, but her head was spinning and her heart was doing flip-flops. The hurt in Antonio's eyes had pierced her like a knife. The bitter irony was that she wanted desperately to be with Antonio this evening, not Drake. But Antonio belonged to someone else, and it was time she accepted that painful truth. Now if only she could convince her heart to let him go.

The next few hours were a blur in Cassie's mind. In spite of the gourmet food and luxurious surroundings of the Blue Ox Restaurant, Cassie's heart and mind remained on Antonio. She listened distractedly and toyed with her food as Drake talked about his life, his work and even the wife and daughter he had left behind. She didn't want to hear this, didn't want to be sucked back into the vortex of Drake's troubled life. She had been burned once too often, and she was determined that it would never happen again.

As they finished their dessert, Drake leaned across the linen-draped table and said quietly, "Have you heard anything I've said tonight, Cassie?"

She lifted a creamy morsel of cheesecake to her lips and said, "Of course, Drake. Every word. Almost."

"But you seem a million miles away. Are you thinking of that man, Antonio, the singer you played for tonight?"

Evasively she asked, "What makes you ask that?"

"I saw the way he looked at you. With the eyes of a man in love."

"Don't be silly," she chided. "He's a married man."

"So was I," Drake said softly.

Cassie tossed him an indignant frown. "Are you suggesting I date only married men?"

"I didn't say that."

"When we were dating I had no idea you were married."

"And your Mr. Paglia...whatever. Did you know he was married?"

Cassie stared down at her plate, tears of shame welling in her eyes. "I must be very stupid to fall for the same trick twice in one lifetime."

Drake reached across the table for her hand. "No, Cass, you're a very lovely woman with a pure heart. I'm sorry you've been hurt this way again. I deeply regret hurting you the first time."

She pulled her hand away. "Then why have you come back? To torment me? To bring back all the pain it took me years to get over? Why are you doing this to me, Drake?"

He laid his fork gently on the china dessert plate. "I'm not sure, Cassie. I made such a mess of my marriage. My ex-wife hates me. She's turned my little girl against me. I guess I just wanted to see if there was anything left of the magic you and I shared."

"There's not," she said solemnly. "You killed my love with your deceit. And now it's happened again, and I'm right back where I was, feeling angry and betrayed and ashamed. I can understand being a fool once. But twice? How could I let it happen again?''

Drake looked genuinely contrite. ''If I could undo what I did to you, Cass, I would. I'd do anything to change the past, to put the bloom of trust and joy back in your face. But I can't. What's done is done. I'm sorry.''

She blinked back her tears. ''Being sorry isn't enough.''

''I know. But…'' Drake drummed his fingers on the table. ''Your father said something tonight in his message that caught my attention.''

She looked at him curiously. ''What?''

''I don't recall the exact words. Something about God loving us while we were still sinners. It blew my mind, the idea that He accepts us just as we are. That He wants to forgive us and give us a clean heart. I always thought I had to clean up my act to get an audience with the Almighty.''

Cassie didn't reply. Was this another tactic of Drake's to gain her sympathy, her affection, her trust? Maybe God was ready to forgive Drake Cameron, but she wasn't.

Later, as Drake drove her back to the church to pick up her car, he said out of the blue, ''I'll be back tomorrow night.''

She stared at him, puzzled. ''Back? Where?''

He flashed an awkward smile, his fingers thrumming the steering wheel. ''The crusade. I'm coming back every night.''

She stiffened. ''Oh, Drake, please don't. I'm not going out with you again.''

"That's okay. I'm not coming for you."

"You're not?"

"No. I want to hear what your father has to say. For the first time in years I see a glimmer of hope. I've got to follow that little beam of light and see where it leads."

Cassie reached for the door handle. "I hope you find what you're looking for, Drake. I hope you do make things right with God. But I can't be there for you. You've got to do it on your own."

He nodded. "I know, Cass. Believe me, I know."

True to his word, Drake Cameron attended the crusade every night that week. Cassie spotted him sitting in the same seat in the third pew. At first she expected him to seek her out after the service and try to wheedle his way into her good graces. But other than complimenting her and Antonio on their performance and exchanging a few pleasantries, he left her alone.

On the last night of the crusade, Cassie and Antonio performed their most ambitious number—selections from Mozart interspersed with classical renditions of traditional hymns. The tone was majestic and passionate, the tempo lively and spirited, and afterward the audience thundered with applause.

Cassie's father was in top form, too, as he delivered one of his most impassioned sermons. From her front row seat, she watched him pace back and forth behind the podium, his eyes ablaze, his ruddy face glistening with a feverish intensity. This was her dad at his best; he was in his element, exactly where he belonged.

"Many of you here tonight think being a Christian means walking around with a sour face and carrying around a burdensome list of dos and don'ts." He demonstrated by wrinkling his brow and turning down his mouth in an exaggerated sad face. "You think God gave us the Ten Commandments because He expected us to keep every single one. Wrong! He already knew we couldn't keep every point of the law. He gave us the Commandments as a mirror so we could see ourselves as we are. So we could see how far short of God's glory we fall.

"He loved us, knowing what flawed creatures we were, knowing we could never meet His standard of perfection. He knew we needed a Savior, so He gave the ultimate gift...His own Son. Jesus paid the price for our sins and conquered death so we could live forever. It's God's free gift to us. We can't earn it. Can't pay for it. All we can do is accept it...open our hearts to Him...and let His Spirit inhabit our lives."

He paused for a moment and rubbed his chin thoughtfully. "It's a win-win situation, you know." The audience remained hushed as Cassie's father sipped a glass of water and wiped his upper lip with his handkerchief. He gazed around the auditorium as if seeking eye contact with each person.

"Think of it!" he boomed, shattering the silence with his resonant baritone. "God created you...and you...every one of you...because He loves you and wants to have fellowship with you. He values you so much, He wants you to experience His love and joy. Imagine, He wants to enjoy you, and He wants you to enjoy Him. Oh, if you had any idea how much the Father loves you!''

He pulled out his handkerchief again and wiped his brow. ''I don't know about you, but when I think about God loving me like that, I get excited. I feel a tingle all the way to my toes. I feel joy in my heart. I feel free of my burdens. I want to bask in love like that. And I want to love Him back. I want to serve Him and please Him and praise Him. I want to be the person He created me to be...and it all starts with simply accepting His gift and opening our hearts to Jesus...''

At the end of the service, as her father invited people to accept God's free gift, Cassie noted that Drake was the first one at the altar, ready to pray. Maybe the Spirit of God had truly touched him. An unsettling, but tantalizing thought crossed Cassie's mind. If Drake Cameron truly was a changed man, did that mean there was a place in Cassie's life for him after all?

Chapter Fourteen

After the service, Cassie glanced around the auditorium, looking for Drake. She wanted him to know how pleased she was for him; surely now God would help him get his life back on track. But before she could find Drake, Antonio strode over and caught her by the arm. "Cassandra, wait. We need to talk."

She looked up warily. "What is it, Antonio?"

A frown creased his brow. "Can't you guess? It's us. It's this tension between us all week. I didn't want to make an issue of it during the crusade. We both had to concentrate on our music. But now it's time to get things out in the open."

"That's an interesting choice of words," said Cassie curtly.

"What do you mean?"

"The idea that you want to get things out in the open now. What about three weeks ago? Three months ago?"

"What are you talking about, Cassandra? You're making no sense."

"I'm making perfect sense."

"Not to me. I don't understand you anymore. We were so close. I thought...I hoped...Cass, what's happened to you...to us?"

She pulled away from his grip and walked out to the vestibule, away from the crowd. She didn't want everyone hearing them argue.

Antonio followed close on her heels. "Wait! Answer me. What's wrong?"

She turned to face him. "Search your heart, Antonio, and I'm sure you'll come up with the answer."

His dusky eyes flashed. "How can I come up with an answer when I don't know what's wrong? When I haven't the slightest idea why you've changed? Why have you grown cold to me, Cassandra, when together we've created the most glorious music? How can you do this to us?"

"How can *you* do this to us?" she returned angrily. "How can you be so selfish and cruel and deceitful to those who love you?"

He stared at her, looking baffled. "What are you saying? How have I been selfish and cruel and deceitful? You say, 'to those who love me.' Who? Are you speaking of yourself? Are you saying you love me, Cassandra? Is it true? Do you love me?"

Tears gathered in her eyes. "And...and what if I do?"

He seized her and drew her into his arms. She could feel the solid warmth of his chest through his starched dress shirt. He ran his fingers through her cascading curls. His voice broke with emotion. "My sweet Cassandra, I have been working on that song I wrote for you. Do you remember?"

She had to be strong, but he was hypnotizing her with his closeness. "Yes, I remember. I—I loved it."

"A silly little song, but I am determined to finish it. When it is done, it will say exactly how I feel."

She looked up and searched his eyes. "How you feel?"

"My darling, don't you know?" His eyes crinkled with merriment. "I love you, just as I know you love me."

"No, Antonio, I never said…"

"You don't have to. I see it in your eyes. I hear it in your voice. I know it in my heart."

She pushed against him, but he held her fast. A few stragglers were milling around, and several eyes were on them, watching curiously. "We can't get into this now, Antonio. Not here."

"Then come with me for a drive. We'll go anywhere you wish. Just say the word."

She shook her head. "There's nothing to talk about."

He tightened his embrace. "There's everything to talk about, Cassandra. Don't you see? We've both been too guarded, too frightened, too set in our ways to admit how we feel. But every night this week, as we sang together I realized I couldn't deny my feelings any longer."

"No, Antonio, don't say it—"

"But I must, Cassandra. I have let my own misgivings inhibit me far too long." He was speaking in a hushed whisper now, obviously aware of the inquisitive onlookers. "I know there are problems to be ironed out, serious matters, but we belong together. I will move heaven and earth to make you mine."

"No, never!" With a sudden surge of strength and resolve, she broke away from Antonio's arms, pivoted sharply...and rushed headlong into the unwitting arms of Drake Cameron. He caught her and stepped back, startled. She drew back, flushed, and uttered a halting apology as she struggled to compose herself. "I'm sorry, Drake, I didn't mean to—"

"I was looking for you, Cass," he said with a twinkle, "but I had no idea I'd run into you so...so dramatically."

Antonio stepped forward, took Cassie's arm, and told Drake with a contrived smile, "We were just on our way out."

"But not together," she corrected. Deliberately she removed Antonio's hand from her arm and approached Drake. "I just wanted to say, I'm happy for you. Taking such a big step of faith. I know God is going to bless you."

"He already has," said Drake softly. "He's brought you back into my life." His brow furrowed slightly. "Not that I'm suggesting anything... I didn't do this for you, I did it for myself. Because it was the right thing to do."

She nodded. "That's the only way it can work."

Drake eyed Antonio, then gazed back at Cassie. "Are you busy? Would you like to help me celebrate over a cup of coffee or a burger? Or steak and candlelight, if you prefer."

"Thank you, Drake. I'll take you up on the coffee," she said, giving Antonio a sidelong glance. She could tell by his expression he was smoldering, wounded. But it was his own fault. She couldn't let herself go on caring for a man who was living a lie. She gave Antonio a small, brittle smile. "Good night."

He held her with his eyes. "We haven't finished our conversation, Cassandra."

"Yes, we have, Antonio," she said with more conviction than she felt. "It's definitely finished." She turned to Drake and said brightly, through a glaze of tears, "I'm ready for that coffee now."

As she and Drake headed for the door, she heard Antonio call after her, "This isn't over, Cassandra. I promise you that. It's only the beginning!"

She straightened her shoulders, tucked her arm in Drake's and kept her gaze straight ahead. For her, it had to be over, and if that meant letting Drake help her forget with some harmless chitchat, so be it.

At breakfast the next morning Cassie's father and sisters were still talking about the crusade. "Wasn't it wonderful?" said Bree as she passed Cassie the scrambled eggs. "I've never heard Daddy sound more eloquent."

Frannie placed a platter of sliced ham on the table and sat down. "I agree with Bree. You were amazing, Daddy."

Her father smiled tolerantly. "Let's give credit

where it belongs. Praise God, He has a predilection for choosing flawed, weak vessels to deliver His truths.''

Frannie leaned over and planted a kiss on her father's brow. ''Well, we're glad He chose you, Daddy, because we never get tired of hearing you talk about the Lord. You always remind us how much He loves us.''

''That's right, Daddy,'' said Bree. ''And you're never stuffy or pompous or boring.''

Frannie turned to Cassie. ''And, sis, you and Antonio were magnificent. When you played and he sang, I felt as if I were standing at the gates of heaven.''

''Thanks, Fran.'' Cassie stared down at her plate. She had to get through this breakfast without letting her sisters see how distraught she was.

''Is that all you can say, Cass?'' quizzed Bree. ''After a week of performing with Antonio, I figured you two would be closer than ever. You are going to keep seeing him, aren't you?''

Cassie blinked her eyes to keep back the gathering moisture. ''No, I don't think so. He has his life…I have mine.''

''And here I thought the two of you had something going,'' said Frannie. ''Well, if you're not interested, maybe I should let him know I'm available.''

Cassie stared back, stunned. ''Don't you dare! He's not the right man for you. He's not right for any of us!''

Frannie held up her palms. ''I was kidding, Cass!''

Cassie relented. "I'm sorry. I didn't sleep very well last night."

Her father gave her a knowing glance. "I noticed you left with Drake Cameron after the service."

She nodded. "We just had coffee together. And a pleasant talk. I think he's really serious about the commitment he made last night. He was actually very nice."

Bree eyed her quizzically. "Are you suggesting you might go back with Drake Cameron?"

Cassie's fingers clenched. "I didn't say that. He's still got a lot of emotional baggage. An ex-wife who won't let him see his only daughter. I don't want to get mixed up in his troubles, but I do care about him and wish him well."

"That brings us back to Antonio," said Frannie. "As far as I can see, he doesn't have any emotional baggage. He's quite a hunk...and smart and talented besides. And he seems to really love the Lord."

"And you," added Bree. "You only have to look at him to see how much he adores you."

Cassie tensed every muscle and still couldn't hold back the tears. "I'm sorry, I can't talk about this!" She pushed back her chair and dashed from the table, finding solace in her father's study.

After a moment he joined her. "Cass, are you okay?" He sat down in the chair beside her. "Is it Antonio?"

She nodded. "He said some things last night... how he feels about me..."

"And...how does he feel?"

Her lower lip quivered. "He says he—he loves me. And...and he thinks I love him."

Her father eyed her intently. "How about it, baby girl? Is he right? Do you love him?"

Cassie's composure crumbled. She put her face in her hands and let the tears flow. "Yes, Daddy, I love him with all my heart."

Her father slipped his arm around her and pressed her head against his shoulder. "Cry it out, honey." He handed her his handkerchief. "You know, when you were a little girl and skinned your knee, I could always find a way to make you feel better. But now the little hurts have turned to big hurts, and only our Heavenly Father has the power to heal those."

"I've tried praying about it, Daddy," said Cassie between sobs, "but I just can't seem to trust the Lord. I keep giving Him my anxieties over Antonio, and then I take them right back again. Why can't I just trust God and believe He'll work all things out for good, like He promises?"

"I have my moments, too, Cassie, when I find it hard to trust God."

She looked up at him through bleary eyes. "You, Daddy?"

He chuckled ruefully. "Yes, me. Oh, I trust God for the big things, like my eternal salvation, but sometimes I have a hard time with the little, everyday things."

"Like what?"

"Like...like my feelings for Juliana. I can't understand why God would let me care about her, when she's obviously not the person I thought she was. I can't figure out what lesson God is trying to teach me.''

''Same here,'' said Cassie. ''I really believed God brought Antonio and Juliana into our lives as a wonderful gift. It all seemed so perfect, like a story-book romance. I guess it was too good to be true.''

''Looks like it, sweetheart. But God will reveal His purpose in all of this, if we wait on Him.''

''I'm trying, Daddy.''

''And you know what you need to do now, don't you?''

Cassie sat back and wiped her eyes and gazed at her father. ''Yes, I know. I wasn't going to see Antonio again, but I need to tell him I know about his wife.''

''His supposed wife.'' Her father gently knuckled her chin. ''Whatever the truth is, Cassie, it's better than going around with all these questions and suspicions eating away at you. Get everything out in the open and see what Antonio has to say.''

Cassie stood up and crossed her arms decisively. ''I will, Daddy. I'll call him this morning. This very minute. But if he's married, I never want to see him again!''

Chapter Fifteen

It took Cassie nearly an hour before she found the courage to telephone Antonio at his home. It was Monday morning. Maybe he had already left for the university. She prayed that he had. Then she could put off confronting him. Probably Juliana would answer. Would she wonder why Cassie was calling? Had Antonio told her of the tension between them?

After five rings, Cassie was about to hang up when she heard someone pick up the receiver. A soft, tentative voice said, "Hello?"

It wasn't Juliana. A maid perhaps? Did they have a maid?

"Who is this?" Cassie asked unthinkingly.

"Belina" came the quiet reply.

"Belina?" Cassie echoed, stunned.

"Yes. Belina Pagliarulo. Who is this?"

"A...a friend of Antonio's," Cassie stammered. Was it possible? She was actually speaking with Antonio's wife?

"Antonio isn't here."

"I—I suppose he's already gone to the university."

"Yes. A half hour ago."

"Is Juliana there?" Cassie asked, for wont of something better to say.

"No, she's not here, either. I'm sorry."

"That's too bad." A daring idea came to Cassie. "I was thinking of stopping by. Do you think Juliana will be gone long?"

"I don't know" came the quiet reply. "Who did you say you are?"

Cassie hesitated. Was there a chance Belina knew who she was? Surely not. "I'm Cass—Cassandra Rowlands."

A long pause, then the woman's voice took on a guarded, bewildered tone: "Are you the woman Antonio's been seeing?"

Cassie's heart pounded. Heaven help her, the poor woman already knew about her relationship with Antonio! "Yes, I am," she confessed miserably. "Please forgive me. I shouldn't have called..."

Belina ignored the implications of Cassie's words. "I'm here alone right now. If you want to come visit, I'm afraid I'm not able to let you in."

"Oh, I wouldn't think of intruding on you."

"You wouldn't be. I think it's time for us to meet."

Suddenly Cassie felt panicky, trapped. "I really don't know if that would be a good idea...."

"But you said you were thinking of stopping by."

"I know, but—"

"There's a key in the flower pot on the porch. Come upstairs to the first room on the right."

Yes, Cassie remembered that room. She could still see Antonio carrying the young woman into that room after their stroll on the beach.

"Are you coming?" asked the mild voice. "We must meet."

Help me, Lord, Cassie prayed silently. *Show me what to do!* "All right. If you're sure that's what you want. I'll be there in a half hour."

As she drove to Antonio's Del Mar estate, Cassie kept telling herself she was crazy to think of confronting Antonio's wife. What was she going to say? What did she expect to accomplish? What if she only made matters worse?

But Belina already knew about her. Maybe Cassie could reassure her that she and Antonio had never had an affair, that he hadn't violated his wedding vows. But he violated them emotionally, she argued with herself. He professed his love for me. That's the greatest betrayal of all. Maybe Cassie couldn't force Antonio to repair his troubled marriage, but she would promise Belina never to see him again. At least then perhaps her own guilt would be assuaged.

Cassie arrived at the estate and walked with growing trepidation up the brick walkway between the two stone lions. On the porch, in a huge blue ceramic vase beside one of the fluted pillars she found the house key and let herself in, her hand trembling. What was she doing here? She felt like a crook, breaking and entering.

Inside the formal entry, she gazed around, listening, in case Antonio or Juliana were home. The enormous house was eerily silent. She climbed the spacious circular staircase, her heart pounding so furiously, surely all the world could hear.

As she reached the top of the stairs and approached the closed door, for an instant she considered running back down the stairs and escaping. But no, she was here now; she had to go through with it.

"Help me, Lord," she whispered. "I want to do the right thing. I trust You to do what's best for all of us."

She knocked lightly on the door. A faint voice inside said, "Come in," so she gingerly turned the brass knob and stepped inside. She caught a glimpse of a pale-pink carpet, a white satin bedspread and lace curtains diffusing golden streams of sunlight. Stuffed animals and dolls in frilly dresses graced the brightly painted shelves. An antique desk and library unit occupied the opposite wall, along with a computer and entertainment center. The room looked like a child's wonderland.

Then Cassie's eyes settled on the diminutive figure silhouetted against the open bay window. The ocean breeze sent the gossamer curtains billowing inward, a diaphanous backdrop to the ethereal young woman dressed in a white satin gown and sitting in a wheelchair. With alabaster skin, shadowed, velvet brown eyes and shiny black hair cascading down over one side of her face, she was breathtaking. And apparently an invalid.

Cassie struggled to find her voice. "Belina?"

"Yes. And you're Cassandra." The girl sat with

her profile to Cassie, as if she didn't wish to look her in the eye. She nodded toward a rose-colored Queen Anne chair to the left of her. "Please. Sit down."

Cassie sat down stiffly, folded her hands, and scoured her mind for what to say next.

Thankfully, Belina broke the ice. "My nurse is usually with me, but she had an emergency at home."

Belina needed a full-time nurse? "Are you all right alone?"

"Yes. I told her to go. I said someone would be home soon. But of course, they won't be home for hours." With long tapered fingers she pulled at a raveling on her gown. "Did you know, they never leave me alone?"

"They—they must care about you very much."

Belina turned her head and gave Cassie a full, scrutinizing glance. Her face had a delicate, not quite real, china doll quality. "Antonio hasn't told you about me, has he?"

Cassie caught her breath. "No."

"That's my doing."

"Your doing? I don't understand."

"It's quite simple, really." Belina spoke in a small, precise voice. "I don't want people to know about me."

Cassie sat forward. She didn't know what to make of this elusive girl...half woman, half child. "Why not?"

Belina looked down at her wheelchair, her long

lashes feathering her cheeks. "Because I'm crippled. I won't have people feeling sorry for me."

"They wouldn't," said Cassie. "I'm sure Antonio is very proud of you."

"Yes, he is." A cryptic smile flickered on Belina's pale lips. "He took me out the other day. To a restaurant. His favorite."

Cassie nodded. She remembered that day very well, could still picture Antonio and Belina sitting cozily together at the Pacific Grille. That was the day Cassie's suspicions began.

"I hadn't been out in months," Belina was saying in her light, breathy voice. "Maybe years. When you stay mostly in one room, time slips away from you, loses its meaning. You don't feel connected to time anymore."

"Most of us are too connected to time," Cassie mused.

"Yes, I feel that way. But not Antonio. He grows restless for me. He can't understand how I can stay here like this day after day. I know I baffle him, frustrate him. I don't mean to."

"Maybe he feels you're missing out on life," ventured Cassie.

"I'm sure he does," Belina agreed with a sad little smile. "He tries to persuade me to go out and face the world again, but I can't. I tried that night. I sincerely tried. But it was too hard. Just being in that restaurant surrounded by people. Shoving, pushing, so close I could hardly breathe. Their eyes watching me. Judging me. Pitying me. I hated it."

"I'm sure Antonio was just trying to help you. He's so caring."

Belina gazed solemnly at Cassie, an unsettling shrewdness in her large, dark eyes. "I know. I live with his solicitude every day of my life. But he doesn't understand. He'll never understand. I should have died a long time ago. I'm already dead... inside."

"But it doesn't have to be that way," Cassie protested. "You have Antonio. This home. His love. You have so much."

"Do I?"

Cassie's face grew warm. She needed to speak, explain herself, assure Belina she wasn't a threat to her marriage. She had to get into this, no matter how much she dreaded it. "I—I don't know what Antonio has told you about me."

Belina picked at her raveling again, as if Cassie's question didn't really interest her. "Very little. Your name. You're a pianist. Quite accomplished, he says. And you performed together. But I know there's more." She paused and looked directly into Cassie's eyes. "I know he brought you here one night."

For a moment Cassie couldn't catch her breath.

"You were here, weren't you?" she asked, too sweetly. "This isn't your first visit."

"No," Cassie admitted. "I was here the night you two were on the beach."

Curiosity flashed in Belina's eyes. "You saw us?"

"Yes." Cassie's mouth felt dry, her tongue pasty. What had she thought she could accomplish in coming here?

"Tell me about that night," urged Belina.

Cassie massaged her knuckles. Her hands were cold with anxiety. "I came over to practice with Antonio, that was all. The fog rolled in...it came off the ocean so suddenly, I didn't dare drive home. So Antonio invited me to spend the night. I assure you, nothing happened. He was a perfect gentleman."

A cryptic smile played on Belina's lips. "Antonio is always a perfect gentleman. Please, go on."

"Well, nothing really. I woke in the middle of the night and couldn't sleep, so I went out on the balcony. The fog had lifted by then. I—I saw Antonio carrying you on the beach."

"Yes, I love the beach," said Belina wistfully. "Especially at night when the breeze is cool and the world is quiet and there's no one else around. Antonio indulges me. He takes me for walks whenever I ask him. But it's always at night. He thinks I am a little daft to love the beach at night, but he humors me. Sometimes he gets up out of a sound sleep to take me out. I think I would go crazy if I couldn't count on him like that."

"I'm glad Antonio is there for you." Cassie's voice shrank to a pained whisper. "That night I—I could see how much he loves you."

Belina nodded, her shiny hair rippling luxuriously over the right side of her face. "He's always been there for me. Especially since the accident." She looked downcast as she added, "But I know I've made his life miserable."

Cassie shifted in her chair. She was feeling more

uncomfortable by the moment. "I'm sure that's not true."

Belina looked up, her eyes wide. "Oh, but it is. Because of me, he hasn't had a life. He blames himself, you know. But it wasn't his fault. I've told him over and over he's not to blame, but he carries the guilt like a terrible burden. I see it in his face. I see the guilt in his eyes when he looks at me."

Belina twisted a strand of hair that fell over her shoulder. "Do you know how hard it is to be with someone who feels that kind of guilt? You want to make it stop, go away, but you can't change anything, because…because that's just how things are."

"Is there anything that can be done?" asked Cassie gently. "Surgery? Physical therapy? Anything to help you walk again?"

Belina let the ringlet fall from her finger. "No. What can anyone do? My spinal cord was severely injured. Years ago I had every kind of test. They poked and probed me until I was black and blue. The doctors kept telling me I should get well, but I never did. After that I vowed I would never see another doctor."

"But there are always new techniques and medical breakthroughs—"

"That's what Antonio says. But he doesn't understand."

"Understand what?"

Belina's dark eyes smoldered. She stroked the shiny mane of hair that covered the side of her face. "He doesn't understand that even if I could walk, I would never leave this room…except for our midnight strolls, of course.''

Cassie stared at her in astonishment. "For heaven's sake, why not?''

Belina continued to stroke her hair, as if she hadn't heard Cassie's question. Cassie asked more forcefully, "Why wouldn't you leave this room, Belina? People in wheelchairs go everywhere these days. They're often very independent people.''

Belina stiffened, her expression tightening with a dark intensity. "No! I'm not like other people. I can never be like others, even if I wanted to be.''

"I don't understand. Why not, Belina?''

"Because of this!'' With a dramatic sweep of her hand, Belina brushed her hair aside, revealing massive scars on the right side of her face. The mottled, discolored blemish ran from her forehead to her chin, stark contrast to the delicate, egg-shell white skin on the left side of her face.

Cassie held back a gasp.

Belina let her hair fall back over her cheekbone. "The accident didn't just paralyze my legs. It destroyed my face, as well.''

"What—what about plastic surgery?'' Cassie asked. She marveled that the disfigurement hadn't touched those beautiful eyes or heart-shaped mouth.

"I've had plastic surgery,'' Belina said darkly.

Cassie shifted in her chair, tears gathering in her eyes. How many more surprises was she going to encounter before she managed to escape this house? "I'm sorry. I—I really shouldn't have come.'' Her voice wavered. "Belina, if I've added to your pain, I hope you'll forgive me."

The girl searched Cassie's eyes with an expression Cassie couldn't quite read. After a minute she said, "Tell me, Cassandra. Are you in love with Antonio?"

The question caught Cassie by surprise. "I—I don't know," she stammered. "But if he had told me about you from the beginning, I never would have allowed my feelings to—"

"Then you do love him?" Belina's slender fingers gripped the arms of her wheelchair. "And I can see every day in his eyes that he cares deeply for you."

Cassie shook her head. "It means nothing. A silly infatuation. Antonio was wrong not to tell me the truth. And I was wrong to let myself care about someone I really didn't know. Now that the crusade is over, I promise never to see him again."

Belina rolled her wheelchair closer to Cassie. "Oh, no, you mustn't. It would break his heart."

Cassie stared at Belina in confusion. "What are you saying?"

Belina's face took on an impassioned animation, her solemn eyes fierce with conviction. "He needs you, Cassandra. Since meeting you he's been happy for the first time in years. I can't let him lose that. Or you."

Cassie stood up. "I don't think you know what you're saying." Obviously Belina was more emotionally unsettled than Cassie had suspected. "I must go. And I meant what I said. I'll have no further contact with Antonio."

"No, you can't do that to him!"

With tears gathering, Cassie strode to the door and gripped the knob. "It's the only way to resolve this terrible mess."

Belina's childlike voice rang out shrill and plaintive. "No, please! He'll hate me. He'll blame me for making you go away!"

Cassie could take no more. Blindly she swung open the door and bolted from the room. She took quick strides across the carpeted landing. The sooner she was out of here, the sooner she could forget that she had ever met Antonio and his baffling family. As she reached the stairs, she heard Belina's wheelchair creaking behind her. She turned, with one hand on the banister, and stared at the distraught young woman. A frail sprite of a figure sitting tall in her chair, Belina looked ghostly in her white gown, her slim hands white-knuckling the wheels.

"You aren't leaving yet, are you?" she asked, as if they had been talking about nothing more than the weather.

"Yes," said Cassie guardedly. "I was wrong to come here. I can see I've upset you."

"No, you haven't." Belina's eyes glinted with a beatific shine. "You've made things clearer for me than they've ever been."

"Clearer? I don't see how…"

Belina wheeled closer to the stairs, hardly a foot from the first step.

"Be careful," warned Cassie.

"Oh, I'm always careful." Belina gazed down the stairwell. "Did you know, sometimes I look at the stairs and imagine myself soaring down them. I can feel myself floating, light as a leaf, free as a bird.'' She held her slender arms out and moved them in a graceful motion, as if they were wings. ''Oh, to be free! Unfettered. Unleashed!''

Cassie's heart pounded in alarm. This visit was becoming increasingly bizarre. ''Belina, please let me take you back to your room.''

Belina laughed ruefully, her gaze still on the stairwell. ''When I was a child, I ran up and down the stairs of our apartment without thinking, taking two steps at a time. It meant nothing to me then. Nothing.'' She gripped the wheels of her chair and sat forward intently. ''Now I would give anything to run and feel the wind on my face and the earth moving beneath my feet.''

Cassie took a furtive step toward Belina. She had to do something to help her without frightening her. ''If you'd like, I'll call Antonio at the university and ask him to come home.''

Belina sat trancelike, her voice slowing, growing remote. ''My world ends at these stairs. I can't go past them except when someone carries me. Do you know how demeaning it is to be a grown woman and be carried like a baby? You feel like a child again, helpless and weak…and a bother. A burden. Because you're not a child. Children grow up someday. Children run and play.''

''You're not a burden,'' Cassie assured her, moving painstakingly closer. ''Not to Antonio. He loves you.''

Belina's fingers moved restlessly over her wheels.

"You wait and see. Someday I'll break free and take the stairs two at a time like I did as a child. I'll run again if it's the last thing I do."

"I'm sure you will...someday." Heaven help her, Belina was irrational, unbalanced. Cassie had to act, now. She seized the chair and wheeled Belina back from the steps. She reached for the brass doorknob and turned it. "I'm taking you back into your room, Belina, and then I'm phoning Antonio. You shouldn't be alone."

Belina twisted her torso and glared back at Cassie. "Leave me alone!" she cried, her voice labored and shrill. "I meant what I said. I would rather die than continue being a burden to Antonio!"

Before Cassie could speak, or react, or even move a muscle, Belina slid her palms vigorously over the wheels, propelling her chair forward across the carpeted landing. It all happened in seconds and yet the horrifying event seemed to transpire in agonizing slow motion...the wheelchair cresting the landing, pitching forward and plummeting down the circular stairs, its metal frame crashing against the wall, splintering the mahogany railing, and bouncing down the steps, until at the bottom of the stairs it spewed out its limp, motionless passenger on the marble foyer.

Chapter Sixteen

Cassie stared down from the landing, appalled. She couldn't move, couldn't breathe. After a moment she shook off her mental paralysis and scrambled down the stairs, her heart pounding furiously.

Please, God, let her be alive!

Belina lay on the cold, hard marble like a floppy, disjointed rag doll, her face white as fine china, her long shiny hair flung back, revealing the purplish, jagged scar, and her slender arms and legs sprawled at odd, frightening angles. Was she breathing? Cassie bent down and felt along her neck for a pulse. It was thready, but it was there. She was still alive!

Cassie got up and looked around for a phone. She found one in the hallway and with trembling fingers dialed 911. "There's been an accident at—at the Pagliarulo estate," she stammered. "Yes, that's the address. Send an ambulance. Hurry!"

The events of the next hour were a frenzied blur.

Somehow Cassie contacted Antonio and Juliana. He was at the university; she was running errands at a nearby shopping mall and had her cell phone with her. They arrived home moments apart, just as the ambulance was about to leave for the hospital with Belina.

Cassie ran to Antonio as he stepped out of his car. He slammed the door and uttered only one word: "Belina?"

"She fell. She's in the ambulance."

Antonio looked at Cassie with an expression of profound scrutiny, as if to ask, *How could you be involved in this?*

She clasped his arm and cried, "I'm sorry, Antonio. I'm so sorry!"

Without replying, he broke away from her and ran to the ambulance. The burly attendant was already ushering Juliana into the back. Holding the door open for Antonio, he said curtly, "Get in now or follow in your car!" Antonio climbed in.

As the ambulance roared away, its siren screaming, Cassie stood alone in the driveway, hugging herself to keep from shaking. Nausea rolled in the pit of her stomach. As she climbed in her car and started the drive home, she realized she was trembling so hard she could barely keep her vehicle on the road. "It's all my fault," she said aloud, fighting tears. "Antonio's wife could be dead, and I'm to blame!"

When she arrived home, she ran inside and burst into her father's study, dissolving in tears. "Oh, Daddy, Daddy!"

He got up from his desk and took her in his arms

and patted her back, the way he always did when she was a child and faced some minor calamity. But this was too big for even him to fix. "What's wrong, Cass?" he urged. "Talk to me!"

Haltingly, still in his arms, she spilled out the whole agonizing story, finishing with, "Now Belina's on the way to the hospital, and, oh, Daddy, I don't know if she's dead or alive!"

Her father released her, grabbed his jacket and reached for his car keys. "Come on, baby. We'll go find out."

On the way to the hospital, Cassie couldn't stop shivering. She massaged her cold, clammy hands, but it didn't help. Over and over she lamented, "It's my fault...all my fault."

"Nonsense," said her father as he accelerated to the speed limit. "You went there to get the truth out in the open. Your motives were decent, honorable."

"Oh, Daddy, I was trying to do the right thing, but I made a mess of everything. I never meant to fall in love with Antonio. I promised Belina I'd never see him again. So why would she deliberately throw herself down the stairs?"

Her father gave her a sidelong glance, his face full of sympathy and love. "One thing I've learned, Cass, honey. No matter what happens in this life, hold on to God. Just hold on tight. He's still in charge. Trust Him, Cassie, no matter what."

She pressed her fists against her quivering lips. "I'm trying, Daddy, but it's so hard."

Within fifteen minutes they arrived at the hospital. While her father parked the car, Cassie hurried inside. She found Antonio and Juliana in the emergency waiting room, Antonio pacing, Juliana sitting in a chair, both looking anxious. A flash of surprise crossed Antonio's face as Cassie ran across the room to him.

"Cassandra, I didn't expect you to—"

"I had to come." She went into his arms. "How is Belina?"

"I don't know. The doctors are examining her now."

"I'm so sorry, Antonio. I shouldn't have gone to see her."

He held her at arm's length and searched her eyes. "Why did you? What happened?"

"We—we were talking. Just talking." Cassie's mouth went dry; she could hardly get the words out. "Suddenly she got this distant look in her eyes, as if she were in another world. And then she—she deliberately pushed her wheelchair down the stairs. Oh, Antonio, I couldn't stop her!"

He gripped her arms tightly. "What were you doing there, Cassandra? How did you know about Belina?"

Cassie's mind raced. She couldn't think clearly. "I—I saw you together at the Grille and walking on the beach. I phoned today and she answered and agreed to meet with me. I wanted to get everything out in the open."

"Where was her nurse? We never leave her alone."

"The nurse had an emergency, so Belina sent her home. She told her you'd be home soon."

Antonio raked his fingers through his tousled hair and looked over at Juliana. "It was a new nurse. She didn't realize Belina can't be left alone."

Juliana shook her head. "I told the nurse to call me if she had to leave for any reason. I told her never to leave Belina!"

Antonio looked back at Cassie, remorse written in his face. "It's my fault. Belina seemed especially troubled today. I shouldn't have left her."

"What's wrong with her?" asked Cassie.

Antonio hung his head. His tormented expression broke Cassie's heart. "What is it, Antonio? Please tell me!"

His voice rumbled with emotion. "Belina is suicidal. We watch her constantly. She's made threats before, even halfhearted attempts. But I never imagined she'd actually harm herself. Never in my wildest dreams…"

Before Antonio could continue, Cassie's father came striding across the waiting room. Expressing his sympathy, he clasped Antonio's arm and embraced Juliana. Juliana began to weep. "Thank you for coming, Andrew," she said, clasping his hand to her lips. "Our poor little Belina needs your prayers. And so do we."

"You have them. I won't stop praying until we know everything's okay." He sat down in the chair beside Juliana and gently massaged her hand. "What did the doctors say?"

Juliana dabbed at a tear. Her hair was mussed and her mascara running, but she still looked stunning. "They're not telling us anything yet. They just whisked Belina away without a word. They won't even let us see her."

"If she wakes and we're not there, she'll be beside herself. Don't they know how much she needs us?" Antonio was pacing again, pummeling his fist against his palm. "I have a good mind to march in there and demand they let us see her."

Cassie clasped Antonio's arm. "Let's sit down. I'm sure someone will come soon."

Antonio looked as if he were about to protest, then with a heavy sigh relented and sat in the chair on the other side of Juliana. Cassie sat beside him. She wondered what to do now. Try to offer comforting words? Hold his hand? Distract him with idle chit-chat. Nothing seemed right, so she sat stiffly, still as a rock, hardly breathing, waiting for news.

Antonio seemed hardly aware she was there. He sat forward and closed his eyes, his elbows on his knees, his chin resting on his folded hands. Maybe he was praying. Or was he turning inward, withdrawing, emotionally distancing himself from Cassie? And why not? She was the reason his wife was in this place, perhaps fighting for her very life.

After a while her father stood up and said, "Can I get anyone some coffee...water...a soft drink?"

Antonio shook his head.

Juliana looked up. "Water, maybe. Thank you, Andrew."

He nodded. "Be right back."

Moments after her father left, Cassie noticed a tall, lean man in a white lab coat approaching. He had a receding hairline and an angular face with piercing black eyes behind wire-rim spectacles. He flashed a small, businesslike smile and offered Antonio his hand. "Mr. Pagliarulo? I'm Dr. Vickery."

Antonio jumped to his feet and seized the physician's hand as if it were a lifeline. "How's Belina?"

"Please, sit down and we'll talk." The doctor pulled a chair over and sat down.

"This is my mother, Juliana," said Antonio, his voice clipped and edgy. "And my friend, Cassandra Rowlands."

The doctor acknowledged their presence with a nod, then turned his attention back to Antonio. "I'm afraid we have little to report at this time, Mr. Pagliarulo. We're still running tests."

"You must know something," Juliana said. "Is it serious? Will Belina be okay?"

"Let's just say we're not out of the woods yet."

"What's wrong with her?" demanded Antonio.

Dr. Vickery cleared his throat. "We suspect some bleeding inside the skull."

Alarm edged Juliana's voice. "Oh, good heavens! That's serious."

Dr. Vickery nodded. "That's why we've sent Ms. Pagliarulo up to radiology."

"Will she need surgery?" Antonio asked. "She's terrified of operations."

"Surgery is a possibility, if there's a heavy bleed. We'll be monitoring her closely for the next forty-eight hours." Dr. Vickery's brow furrowed. "We do have some questions about how Ms. Pagliarulo was injured."

"My mother and I weren't there," Antonio said.

"I was there," said Cassie. "I'll tell you whatever I can."

"Fine. We'll have reports to file. But we can talk about that later." He glanced at the chart in his hands. "I'd also like to contact Ms. Pagliarulo's family physician and review her previous medical records."

"She has no doctor," Juliana stated.

"No doctor? Who treated her for her spinal cord injury?"

"That was many years ago," Antonio replied. "For several years after she was injured she underwent every conceivable test, until she'd had enough. The doctors kept expecting her to improve, but she didn't. After a while, she lost hope. Since then, she's refused any treatment whatsoever."

Dr. Vickery rubbed his narrow jaw thoughtfully. "Does she realize there have been amazing advancements in spinal cord treatment in the last few years?"

"Are you saying...Belina could walk again?"

"I'm just saying she owes it to herself to see a specialist and learn about the latest medical techniques. I would also suggest she investigate the latest breakthroughs in plastic surgery for her facial scars. I suspect she's been living in the Dark Ages far too long."

Antonio nodded. "I'll try to convince her."

"But right now we must concentrate on her current condition. When she returns from radiology, I'll let you see her for a few minutes. But don't tire her. She's still a very sick girl."

Antonio sat forward intently. "But you do expect

her to recover, don't you? My sister is going to be okay?''

"We'll do everything we can for her," Dr. Vickery said as he stood up and closed the chart. With a compassionate nod toward Juliana, he turned and walked away.

He was just out of hearing distance when Cassie blurted in astonishment, "Your *sister?*" She sat bolt upright and stared at Antonio. "Belina is your sister?''

Antonio stared back with a perplexed frown. "Yes, of course. My sister. Who did you think she was?''

"Your wife!" exclaimed Cassie. "I thought she was your wife!''

"My wife?" trumpeted Antonio. "How could you think that?'' He broke into a hearty guffaw that quickly dissolved into furious indignation. He stood to his full height and stared down at Cassie, his hands on his hips. "You thought I was married? What kind of a man do you think I am?''

Shame and humiliation burned Cassie's cheeks. "I saw you with her at the restaurant and on the beach. She was living in your house with you. What else was I supposed to think?''

"Think? Think nothing! If you didn't know, why didn't you ask me? All you had to do was ask!''

Cassie stared up at Antonio, hot tears scalding her cheeks. "Why didn't you tell me about Belina? If you loved me, why didn't you tell me the truth?''

"What truth?" challenged Antonio. "My sister was my business. She had nothing to do with us!''

"She had everything to do with us," Cassie protested. "You kept a big part of your life secret from me. You didn't trust me enough to tell me about her, so I drew my own conclusions."

"And you didn't trust me enough to voice your suspicions! You chose to believe the worst about me. How could you say you loved me when you believed I was betraying my poor bedridden wife? I'll say it again. What kind of man do you think I am, Cassandra?"

"I don't know. I guess I didn't know you, after all."

"And I obviously didn't know you, either."

Juliana sprang to her feet and stepped between Cassie and Antonio. "I will not have the two of you arguing like silly children when my daughter is lying in a hospital bed, broken in body, broken in spirit. We must put aside our own petty complaints and differences and rally around Belina. She needs us now as never before!"

Antonio heaved a shuddering sigh. "You're right, Mama. All we should think about now is Belina and making her well."

Isn't that all you've ever done? Cassie wondered as she gazed at Antonio and Juliana. *You let Belina become a recluse. You smothered her with care, when all she really wants is to be free. Someday I'll dare to tell you so.* Cassie met Antonio's gaze, but he was still glowering at her with his righteous indignation.

Suddenly, she realized with heart-stopping clarity that every assumption she had made about this man was wrong in light of this new revelation. Belina was his sister. His sister! Not his wife! That single truth changed everything. And yet, by the disapproving look on Antonio's face, it was obvious that truth had come too late.

Chapter Seventeen

Andrew arrived back in the waiting room with Juliana's glass of water just in time to witness one of the strangest brouhahas he had ever encountered. It wasn't a knock-down, drag-out fight, but the tension in the room was so thick it could have been sliced like cheese and passed around. Cassie, Antonio and Juliana were all talking at once with excitement bordering on hysteria, and not one was listening to the others.

"What's going on here?" Andrew boomed as he took his seat beside Juliana and handed her a glass of water.

They looked at Andrew for an instant of stark silence and then all replied at once, like a cacophonous chorus.

"Daddy, Belina is Antonio's sister, not his wife," exclaimed Cassie.

"She's my daughter, Andrew," said Juliana. "I

should have told you, but I never dreamed there would be such a huge misunderstanding!''

"Your daughter believed I was married!'' countered Antonio. "What kind of lowlife did she think I was...dating her, with a sick wife at home!''

"Whoa! Let's count to three and start over,'' Andrew admonished. He had to do something. The situation was deteriorating rapidly. "It looks like we all have some explaining to do...and maybe some apologizing and forgiving.''

"I don't know.'' Antonio sounded dubious; his expression was grim. "I think maybe it's too late for that.''

"It's never too late for forgiveness,'' said Andrew, with more courage than he felt. "I'll start the ball rolling. I'm sorry, Antonio and Juliana, that I didn't come to you the first time I had questions, to get it all out in the open. Instead, I let my suspicions fester. And, Juliana, I tried playing mind games to get you to tell me what I believed was the truth. I was wrong. Will you forgive me?''

Juliana patted his hand. "You are forgiven, Andrew.''

"It's not just Daddy's fault,'' Cassie said, nervously clenching her hands. "I made him promise not to tell you what we suspected. I'm the one to blame.'' She gazed at Antonio. "I'm sorry. I didn't trust you enough to confront you with my suspicions. I was afraid of the truth. Afraid of losing you. Afraid of being hurt.''

Andrew reached over and clasped his daughter's hand and gave her a smile that said, *Good girl!* Then he cast a quizzical glance at Antonio. "What do you say? Can we forgive and forget?"

Antonio looked at Cassie with shadowed, brooding eyes. "I wondered why you had changed, Cassandra, why you were acting so remote. I thought it was because you were beginning to care again for that other man. Drake...Drake Cameron. During the crusade, when you left with him, I knew I was losing you."

"But you weren't. Not really. It's just that I—"

"That you never really knew me. Because if you had known the man I am, you wouldn't have believed such unspeakable things about me."

Cassie began to weep. "I'm sorry, Antonio. I was wrong not to tell you my suspicions. Will you forgive me?"

He rubbed the back of his neck, his brow still furrowed. "It's easy to toss words around. *Forgive. Forget.* But what do they mean? Do they really change anything? I can say I forgive you and ask you to forgive me, but the truth is, we are not the people we thought we were, or we would not be in this painful predicament."

"But we can start with forgiveness," said Cassie. "It's a beginning."

"She's right," said Andrew. "We all need to start over with one another. A fresh start. A clean slate. How about it?"

Antonio nodded, but Andrew could still see a reluctance in his face. Apprehension, wariness. He was still holding something back. "If you need time, Antonio, we don't want to push, but I have the feeling that everything's not on the table, that there's more to be said.''

Antonio rubbed his jaw, his gaze on the distant wall.

''What is it?'' Cassie urged. ''Is there something else we need to know?''

Antonio cracked his knuckles, one hand, then the other. ''I'm not guilty of unfaithfulness...but I have lived with guilty feelings for most of my life.''

Cassie stared at him. ''Guilt? Why?''

Juliana pressed her palm over her son's hand and said ruefully, ''He has never let this go. God knows I have told him over and over he's not to blame.''

''Blame for what?'' Andrew asked gently. ''What are you blaming yourself for, Antonio?''

A tendon throbbed along his temple and his mouth twisted as he uttered, ''My sister's condition. Her paralysis. Her scars. I did that to her!''

''No, Antonio, you didn't!'' Juliana cried. ''You were just a little boy. You meant no harm. It was your father! His drinking! He never should have been driving.''

Andrew turned to Juliana. ''You're talking about the car accident that killed your husband?''

She put her face in her hands. ''Yes, my husband died...and my daughter was burned and crippled.''

Cassie slipped her hand over Antonio's. ''If your father was driving, why do you blame yourself?''

He stared off into space. ''It's a long story.''

''We have time,'' said Andrew. ''The doctor said it'll be awhile before we can see your sister. Why don't you tell us?''

Antonio cleared his throat and said huskily, "That night was the most tragic, defining moment of my life. I was ten years old. Belina was eight." He shook his head and closed his eyes.

"It's okay, Antonio," said Cassie softly. "I remember you telling me about that night. You were on vacation in the Catskill Mountains."

He nodded. "We were driving around some hairpin curves. My father had been drinking, as usual. Belina and I were sitting in the back seat. We could hear our parents arguing."

Juliana broke in. "I begged Marco to slow down or let me drive, but he wouldn't. He roared back and said, 'You think you can handle a car better than I can? Sure you can. You can do anything better. Sing, hold down a job, bring in a paycheck. You can do it all!' But that wasn't true. I needed him. His children needed him. But he couldn't see that."

Juliana began to weep softly. "Why couldn't he see how much we all loved him?"

Andrew slipped his arm around Juliana's shoulder. This was one of those times when there was nothing he could say; his sentiments could only be expressed with an embrace.

"As my father's temper rose, his speed increased," Antonio continued. "Belina started crying, whimpering, begging our father to slow down. 'Daddy, please, please, let Mommy drive.' I was scared, too, but I didn't want to admit it, so I started calling my sister, 'Crybaby, crybaby!' We began to scuffle, the way brothers and sisters do at that age." Antonio's voice shook with emotion. "The—the last thing I remember is my father looking around at us and shouting, 'Will you two kids shut up!'"

Antonio brushed at moisture on his eyelids. "The next thing I knew I was waking up in a hospital room and every muscle in my body hurt. I kept calling for my mother. The nurses told me she was in another room and would come see me soon."

"Thank God, I had only a broken arm and several cracked ribs," Juliana said, her voice hushed and emotion filled. "Antonio and I were released from the hospital within a few days."

"It wasn't until then I learned my father had died in the crash. And my sister...well, you know what happened to her."

"And you convinced yourself the crash was your fault," Andrew observed, his own emotions rising. "All these years you've carried that burden, that guilt?"

Antonio nodded. "If I just hadn't distracted my father that night, maybe he'd still be alive. Maybe he would have sobered up eventually, changed his life. Maybe we would have had a chance to know each other. Maybe my sister could have lived a happy, fulfilled life."

Cassie squeezed his hand. "Please, Antonio, you can't keep living with recriminations and guilt. You've got to let go and forgive yourself. Let God help you."

"Oh, I made my peace with God a long time ago." Antonio raked his fingers through his dark hair. His voice took on a distant, detached tone, as if he were looking inward at something no one else could see. "I know God has forgiven me. But always in my mind there's a black hole that threatens to suck me in. It's the memory of my father and our last minutes together. In my dreams I keep seeing our automobile careening over a cliff, plummeting into darkness, with the screams rising around me, echoing eerily in the night, like something out of a horror movie.

"I never hit the ground in my dream. I just keep falling helplessly through this endless black vortex toward death. Sometimes I wake up in a cold sweat, and I know the next night the dreams will start all over again. So even though God has forgiven me, I can never quite forgive myself."

Juliana tucked her hand protectively around her son's arm. "That is the reason Antonio has never allowed another person into his life. He has never let anyone get close to him, not even me, his own mother, and surely not a woman who might fall in love with him and want to know his inner heart. So he lives with this terrible barricade around himself, and won't let anyone inside."

"That's not so, Mama," Antonio scoffed. He gave Andrew a mirthless grin. "Mama's being her usual melodramatic self."

"My Tonio, I am not," Juliana protested. "You have always had a wall around you. That is why I was so pleased when you began to care for Cassandra. I knew you had found the one woman who could unlock your emotions and help you live again."

Antonio sprang to his feet, breaking free from both Cassie and Juliana. "This is enough! All the talking in the world won't change anything. My sister is lying alone and broken somewhere in this hospital. She could be dying, and we sit here talking about irrelevancies!''

Andrew got up and followed Antonio across the room. He gripped his shoulder in a small gesture of camaraderie. ''She'll be all right, Antonio. I sincerely believe it.''

Antonio ground his jaw, his mouth tightening to a jagged line. Andrew could see that he was struggling hard to keep a grip on his emotions. ''You're a man of God, Andrew,'' Antonio said after a tremulous moment, ''and faith is your stock in trade. Sometimes I feel as if I'm still at square one with God. I'm not sure He wants to do me any favors.''

Andrew tightened his grip on Antonio's shoulder. ''That's where you're wrong, my boy. God has already given us the favor of His grace, the gift of His Son. Anything after that is frosting on the cake.''

Before Antonio could reply, Dr. Vickery came striding through the double doors of the emergency room. ''Mr. Pagliarulo, your sister has just been taken up to her room.'' He glanced down at his chart. ''She's on the second floor, Room 210. You and your mother may go see her now.''

''How's she doing?'' Antonio asked, all of his energies suddenly focused on the wiry physician.

''So far so good. She's beginning to respond favorably. Now all we can do is wait and see what the tests and X rays reveal.''

''Thank you, Doctor.''

"Keep your visit short. We don't want to tire her."

After Antonio and Juliana left to visit Belina, Andrew sat down beside his daughter and heaved a weary sigh of relief. "Been quite a day, huh, muffin?"

Cassie nestled close to her father. "Oh, Daddy!" No other words came.

Andrew gave his daughter a reassuring hug. "God is in this, honey. I feel it. He's doing a special work in all of us."

Cassie laid her head on his shoulder. "I know, Daddy. I just wish it didn't hurt so much."

"You think you've lost Antonio for good?"

"Don't you? His pride is so wounded."

"Pride's one of those things most of us have too much of anyway. Pride usually just gets us into trouble."

"But he's right. We really don't know each other very well."

"Well, don't give up on him yet. He may surprise you."

She looked up at him, her eyes searching his. "What about you and Juliana?"

He hedged. "What about us?"

"You care about her, don't you?"

"Sure. She's a good friend."

"No, Daddy, I know better than that. And I know she has feelings for you."

"Whatever either of us might have felt—and I'm not admitting to a thing, mind you—I'm sure from now on Juliana will be devoting herself entirely to her daughter.''

''You're right, Daddy.'' Cassie managed a crooked little smile. ''So it looks as if both of us have struck out in the romance department.''

Andrew ruffled his daughter's tousled curls. ''No, baby girl, not by a long shot. The Rowlands clan never strikes out. We're going to come through this winners yet. You wait and see!''

A spontaneous smile broke on Cassie's lips. ''So what do we do now, Daddy?''

He inhaled deeply. ''Tell you what. I'm going to phone my secretary and ask her to clear the dockets for me for the next few days.''

''You're going to clear your calendar? Why?''

''So I can hang around here in these antiseptic halls…just in case Juliana needs a sturdy shoulder to lean on.''

''Other than Antonio's, you mean?''

''Right! And I'd like to spend some time with that troubled young daughter of hers. Praying…listening. Let her know people care…and we're here for her.''

''Daddy, you're the greatest!'' Cassie sat up straight and squared her shoulders. ''I'm staying, too,'' she said decisively. ''No matter how angry Antonio is with me, even if he never speaks to me again, I'm going to be here for him. And for Belina.''

Cassie looked up with a faraway glint in her eyes. ''You know, Daddy, I felt a strange sort of connection with Belina when we talked at her house today. She seemed so lonely and sad. I wanted to reach out to her, do something to make her life happier, better.

But I didn't understand where she was coming from. I felt powerless to help her. But maybe God will still give me that chance. If He does, I'm going to do everything I can to help her get well.''

"A worthy goal, Cass!" Andrew gave his daughter a quick bear hug and kissed the top of her head. Awhile back he had felt as if his capacity for deep emotion had died with Mandy, but the way he was feeling right now, he knew that wasn't so. His voice resonated with hope and conviction, as he declared, "Looks like we've got our work cut out for us, baby girl."

Chapter Eighteen

Cassie had just hit the snooze button on her alarm and rolled back over, hugging her pillow, when the bedside phone rang. She fumbled for the receiver and licked her dry lips, trying to clear the cobwebs of sleep from her brain. "Hello?" she said thickly.

"Cassandra?" Antonio's voice came over the line.

Cassie sat bolt upright, her heart racing. "Antonio? Is it Belina? Is she okay?"

"I thought you and your father would want to know. We finally got all the reports. It took several days for the last ones to come in. I'm sorry, did I wake you?"

"No…yes…it doesn't matter. What did they say?"

"Good news. Tests showed no residual bleeding in her skull. And everything else has checked out, too."

"Then she's going to be okay?"

"Looks that way. The doctors are optimistic. They want to keep her for a few more days just to be on the safe side. But barring no complications, she should be able to go home in time for Thanksgiving."

"What a perfect time. Thank God!" Cassie blinked back a sudden rush of tears. "I'm so happy for all of you."

"There's more, Cassandra. The doctors want Belina to begin physical therapy. They think there's a good chance she could walk someday."

"Oh, Antonio, that's what you've prayed for for years."

"More years than I care to remember." Antonio's voice took on a solemn note. "Belina will also have to undergo psychological counseling. She admitted to her doctors that she deliberately rolled her wheelchair down the stairs."

"I'm glad she told them," said Cassie quietly. "Now she can get the help she needs."

"Actually, our whole family will be participating in the counseling."

"That's probably best."

"Your father's agreed to be involved, too, Cassandra. Did he tell you that?"

"He did mention it. I'm glad."

"He's been there for me the past few days the way I wish my father could have been. Talking... listening...praying...reading the Scriptures with me. I feel as if I'm waking out of a long sleep, as if I've been set free with Belina."

"That's wonderful, Antonio." Cassie paused,

searching for the right words. "I hope you understand why I haven't been up to the hospital for the past few days. They would only allow the immediate family to see Belina…and my father, of course, since he's a minister. And, knowing how you feel, I thought maybe it was better we not see each other right now. That is how you feel, isn't it, Antonio?"

That wasn't what she wanted to say at all. It sounded as if she was the one who didn't want to see him, when she was really hoping he would insist she come over. But it was too late to retract her words.

"If that's how you feel, Cassandra." Antonio's voice cooled perceptibly. "There's no reason you should feel obligated to see any of us. I'm sure you're very busy these days."

"That's not what I meant, Antonio. I want to come—"

"You don't have to explain, Cassandra." Antonio paused for a moment, then said briskly, "Well, I just wanted to call and let you know about Belina. I'd better get back to her."

"Wait, Antonio." Cassie took a steadying breath. "I don't think you understand. I really do want to see your sister. Would you let me know when they allow visitors outside the family?"

Antonio's voice was coolly reserved. "I'm sure you can see her whenever you like, Cassandra."

"Really?" Cassie hesitated. That first day she had felt eager to help Belina, but then her fears took over. She couldn't bring herself to face Antonio. "My father will be coming to the hospital later this morning. Maybe I'll come with him.''

"All right. I'm sure Belina will want to see you.''

"And what about you, Antonio?'' ventured Cassie. "Do you mind my coming?''

"Why should I?'' His voice remained cool, detached. "But, as I said, don't feel you have to come for my sake.''

"I don't,'' she said quickly, a knot of disappointment tightening in her chest. "I want to be there.''

"Fine. I'll see you later, then.''

"Goodbye, Antonio.'' With huge tears rolling down her cheeks, Cassie hung up the receiver and burrowed back under the covers. Obviously, Antonio had no desire to see her, and certainly no wish to rescue their floundering relationship. If he had ever loved her, that love had been snuffed out by her mistrust and suspicions.

Cassie sat up in bed and hugged her knees to her chest. She felt suddenly like an abandoned child, heartbroken and alone. "Dear God,'' she whispered into the stillness, "I've made such a mess of things, but I know You still love me and forgive me. Lord, I've been so busy trying to accomplish my own agenda with Antonio, that I forget You might be trying to show me another path. You know how stubborn and pigheaded I can be. Please don't let my willfulness collide with Your will for me. Help me to see things through Your eyes. Help me to be Your obedient child, even if it means losing Antonio forever. And let me remember that even if I lose everyone I love, I still have You, dear God.''

And now it was time to put aside her own heartaches and focus on Belina and her needs, even if the
idea of going to the hospital and facing Antonio
struck terror in her heart. How could she face him
again, knowing how disappointed he was in her? But,
God help her, she would do it somehow!

She climbed out of bed, threw on her robe and
headed for her father's room to give him Antonio's
report. Her father would probably want to drive to
the hospital directly after breakfast.

Cassie had no sooner returned to her own room to
shower and dress than the phone rang again. *Maybe
Antonio forgot to tell me something.* She picked up
the receiver, expecting to hear Antonio's voice and
did a double take when she recognized the familiar
voice of Drake Cameron.

"Drake, how are you?" she inquired with one eye
on the clock. She had to make this short if she was
to be ready in time.

"Cass, I need to see you. Are you busy tonight?"

"Tonight? I—I don't know. What is it, Drake?"

"I don't want to talk about it over the phone, Cass.
Please, say you'll see me. Now that I have my life
straightened out with God, it's time for me to repair
some broken relationships. I need to start with you."

He wants to get back together! Cassie thought,
butterflies of panic fluttering in her stomach. "I don't
know if that's a good idea, Drake. I'm awfully busy
this week."

"It has to be soon, Cass. I'm leaving town next
week, and I can't go until we've talked."

"All right," she said uncertainly. "Pick me up tonight."

"Six okay? I thought we could have dinner together."

"Dinner? All right. I'll see you tonight."

On the way to the hospital Cassie's father noticed how preoccupied she was. "Thinking about Antonio?" he asked.

"No," she confessed. "I'm thinking about Drake." She told him of his phone call and their date tonight.

"Dinner, huh? What if he wants to get back together?"

"I don't know, Daddy. Now that Antonio is out of the picture..."

"Then you'd seriously consider going back with Drake?"

Cassie thought about it. What an easy solution it would be. Extinguish her heartache over Antonio in the flames of a fresh romance with Drake, a man who had held her heart captive for several years. It seemed to make sense. Drake was unattached now, and a Christian. What was there to keep them apart?

The thought struck her like a sudden gust of wind: *Trust in the Lord with all your heart; don't lean on your own understanding. Let God direct your path...*

"Daddy, I don't know what I'll do about Drake," she replied at last, "but I want to choose the way God has for me. Pray that He'll give me wisdom... and that I'll follow where He leads."

Her father's eyes twinkled. "Darling, I've been

praying that prayer for you for over twenty-six years!''

At the hospital, Cassie had little time to think about a possible future with Drake. The moment she entered Belina's room and saw Antonio and Juliana standing by her bed, Cassie felt a flood of contradictory emotions...joy and anxiety, hope and fear, sorrow and love. She hadn't realized how much she cherished her friendship with Antonio and his mother until now that she risked losing it.

With clammy palms and a pounding heart Cassie approached Belina's bedside and offered a smile. The fragile woman looked pale and childlike in the huge bed with its iron rails, and her ebony hair was feathered out on the pillow, revealing the puckered, purplish scar along her cheekbone. But her large, expressive eyes were bright and the hint of a smile played on her ashen lips.

''Hello, Cassandra. We meet again,'' she said in a small, breathy voice.

Cassie moved closer and touched Belina's delicate hand. ''Yes, and I'm so glad you're feeling better. You had us all very worried.''

Belina smiled wistfully. ''I tried to soar to another world...and I ended up here. But Antonio says the hospital is the best place for me now. He thinks they can help me walk again. And maybe even fix my scar someday. But even if they can't, he says I can be free inside. In my heart. In my spirit. He says he'll help me.''

''So will I, 'Lina,'' Juliana said as she massaged her daughter's forehead.

"I'd like to help, too, if I could," Cassie added.

Her father stepped forward and offered Belina his hand. "I think that makes it unanimous, young lady. We're all here for you."

Later that afternoon, as Cassie and her father prepared to leave the hospital, Antonio stopped them in the lobby. "Andrew, Cassandra, wait up. I'd like a word with you."

Cassie turned and gazed up into Antonio's vivid, brown eyes, and for a moment her heart stopped. She could swim and drown in those eyes, lose herself in them forever.

Her father's voice broke her reverie. "What is it, Antonio? A problem with your sister?"

"No, on the contrary." Antonio's sturdy face glistened; his eyes shone with an odd merriment. "I just want to thank you again for coming. For being here for Belina. I can see already that she adores you, Cassandra. I know you're going to play a big part in her recovery."

"I—I hope so," said Cassie in a small, guarded voice. Was that all Antonio felt for her now? Gratitude?

"And, so, I just wanted to say…thanks. Thank you both. You don't know what your concern means to my mother and me." Antonio rubbed the back of his neck, as if he'd run out of words and didn't quite know how to break off the conversation.

"We'll be back tomorrow as usual," her father stated. "Bright and early."

"Not too early," Cassie said. "I have a date tonight." Merciful heavens, what had prompted her to blurt that out? Was she so desperate to make Antonio jealous that she'd stoop to baiting him? If so, it worked.

"A date?" he inquired, his eyebrows arching. "With Drake, I suppose."

"Yes. Drake Cameron. He says he has something important to tell me." In the name of heaven, what was she doing, telling Antonio this?

Antonio stepped back, almost in a gesture of retreat, his face darkening. Politely he said, "I hope your evening is everything you want it to be, Cassandra. Good night, Andrew."

That evening, as Cassie waited for Drake to arrive, she brooded over her parting words to Antonio. Surely now he assumed she was planning a future with Drake. There would be no chance for her to make amends with the man she truly loved.

"Maybe Drake is the man I'm meant to be with after all," she murmured as she twisted her ash-blond hair in a chignon and feathered little curls along her cheekbones. "Lord, I'm always running headlong into trouble. Please show me the way. Your way!"

Drake drove her to a quaint little Italian restaurant in Del Mar. But why Italian? she wondered. It reminded her painfully of Antonio! She ordered spinach cannelloni and he ordered shrimp scampi, and he proposed a toast with crystal glasses of sparkling water. "To the future. May we both find the path that God has set before us."

"To the future," she echoed weakly. But would it be fair to marry Drake on the rebound? And how could she tell him they couldn't share a future together unless God gave her peace about it?

"You look very thoughtful tonight," Drake observed as he handed her a basket of garlic bread.

"And you seem very upbeat and happy," she noted.

"Why shouldn't I be?" His ruddy face nearly beamed. He ran his palm over his slick black hair. "My life is finally on course, and I have the joy of the Lord in my heart."

"I'm glad for you," said Cassie. "You've had a rocky journey these past few years."

"Most of it of my own making. I made a lot of bad choices. Hurt a lot of people. But all of that is in the past. From now on life is going to be beautiful…because God is in charge."

"It's wonderful you feel that way," Cassie conceded, "but that doesn't mean there won't still be, uh, problems. Disappointments."

"Oh, I realize that. But this time, when the troubles come, I know who to take them to. I won't have to face them alone."

She nodded her agreement. "That's right. No matter what, you have the Lord."

He grinned. "Thanks to you, Cassie. You're the one who invited me to your father's crusade. I owe you a lot."

She shook her head. "You don't owe me…."

He reached across the table for her hand. "Yes, I do, Cass. I owe you for the lousy way I handled our relationship years ago. I lied to you, deceived you, was ready to violate my marriage for my own selfish pleasures. I hurt you, I hurt my wife, I hurt my daughter. I can never undo what I did. I can only ask forgiveness and assure you I'm a different man today.''

"I know that, Drake. I can see it in your face, hear it in your voice, witness it in your life. I'm proud of you.''

"Then I hope you'll be pleased with what I'm about to do.'' He tightened his grip on her hand.

She wanted to pull away, felt a sudden desperation to get up and run. She wanted to shout out, I'm sorry, Drake, I can't marry you; I love another! But she kept her silence and held her breath, waiting, nervous as a kitten on a wire.

"I'm going home, Cass.''

"Home?''

"Back to my wife and daughter. I'm getting married again.''

"Married?'' Cassie was dumbstruck. She couldn't quite collect her thoughts. Drake was talking about marriage, but he hadn't proposed to Cassie. "You—you're going to remarry your wife?''

"If she'll have me.'' Drake was beaming. "I wasn't even sure she'd see me, let alone take me back, but I've been talking to her on the phone the past few weeks. I told her about getting right with God, and, well, would you believe? She's willing to give me another chance. So I'll be driving home in a few days. If all goes well, there'll be wedding bells soon.''

"Wedding bells!'' Cassie still couldn't quite process this new information. But one truth was settling in. She didn't have to worry about turning down Drake's marriage proposal, because he wasn't offering one! Suddenly everything was falling into place in perfect order, and she felt a sweeping sense of relief. "Oh, Drake," she enthused, "I couldn't be happier for you! I think you're doing exactly the right thing!"

He nodded, still grinning ear-to-ear. "I know I am, Cassie. And before I left town, I wanted to make sure things were right between us. I need to know I'm forgiven. And I want you to know how grateful I am that, after all I did to hurt you, you still cared about my soul. That's true, godly love."

Cassie's face grew warm. She wasn't sure Drake's praise was well deserved. But she was thankful God had used her, even if her motives were sometimes flawed.

The next morning, when Cassie and her father arrived at the hospital, Antonio was waiting in the lobby for them. "Is something wrong with Belina?" Cassie asked.

"No, she's doing fine." He broke into a grin. "In fact, the doctors have called in several neurological and orthopedic specialists. They'll be examining her today. It's looking more and more like Belina may not have to spend the rest of her life in a wheelchair."

"Then why aren't you in her room celebrating?" asked Cassie.

Antonio shifted from one foot to the other. "I will, Cassandra, but first, I wanted to talk to you." He gave her father a cryptic glance. "Do you mind, Andrew? I'd like to talk to your daughter alone."

Cassie's father gave him a knowing smile. "I don't mind at all, Antonio. I'll go on upstairs and visit with your mother and sister."

Antonio took Cassie's elbow and ushered her down the hall. "We'll go to the cafeteria, if that's all right. The food is lousy, but I'm not hungry anyway."

"Me, neither," said Cassie. "I just had breakfast."

Antonio found a back corner table in the large, noisy room, amid the bedlam of voices, where the clink of silverware and trays punctuated the monotonous din of conversation. Even here there was that lingering antiseptic smell mingling with the heavy aromas of sausage and coffee.

Antonio went through the line and brought back coffee and pastries and set them on their small orange, molded plastic table. He sat down across from her and offered her sugar and cream. She took them unthinkingly and poured them into her coffee and stirred it. At last she found the courage to look Antonio in the eye and ask, "What did you want to talk to me about?"

He sipped his coffee, a morose expression around his eyes. "It's probably too late."

"Too late for what?"

He gazed down at her ring finger. "I suppose you're already engaged."

"Engaged?" This conversation was growing more bizarre by the moment. "Engaged to whom?"

"Drake. Drake Cameron. You said he had something to ask you."

"No, I said he had something to *tell* me."

"Same difference." With an odd, restless energy Antonio turned his coffee mug between his palms. "I suppose he mentioned marriage."

Cassie smiled. Why not play along? "Well, now that you mention it, he did."

"I knew it! He proposed, didn't he!"

"Not exactly," she said coyly.

"What do you mean? He either did or he didn't!"

She sipped her coffee, wondering how long she dared draw this out before Antonio got annoyed. Obviously, not long!

He sat forward resolutely, his fists clenched. "Are you marrying that man, Cassandra?"

She met his gaze unflinchingly. "Drake plans to get married, but not to me. He's going back to his wife."

The truth seemed to take all the starch out of Antonio's wrath. He sank back in his chair and expelled a huge sigh. "Back to his wife? Really? That's good. He's doing the right thing." He paused suddenly and gazed at Cassie, raising one eyebrow. "How do you feel about that? I know you cared for him. Are you okay?"

She nodded. "I'm fine. I think he's following God's leading."

"Then you're not upset?"

"No." She gazed down at her coffee. She wanted to say, I'm not upset about Drake, but I am in a tailspin over you.

"Well, I'm glad. I never did think that man deserved you."

Cassie dabbed at a water ring on the table. "It's a moot point now, isn't it?"

"I suppose so." Antonio tugged at his shirt collar. It was a light-blue knit shirt with some kind of emblem on the pocket. The shirt accented his muscled chest and the breadth of his shoulders. Even in casual clothes, he possessed an aristocratic air. Cassie waited for him to speak again, and when he didn't, she broke the silence. "What is it you wanted to talk to me about, Antonio?"

He drummed his fingers on the tabletop. "I—I wanted to apologize for my behavior lately."

"Your behavior?"

"Since I learned you thought I had a wife, I've been acting like a spoiled child. My pride was hurt. I thought you knew me better than that. But considering how Drake deceived you, I understand why you would be suspicious of me. But now that I've had time to think about it, I realize you had some valid reasons for your suspicions. I also realize if I had just told you about my sister in the first place, we wouldn't have had this entire misunderstanding."

Cassie sat forward attentively. "Why didn't you tell me, Antonio? There's no shame in having a handicapped sister. Why did you allow her to stay hidden all these years?"

He shook his head ponderously. "I honestly don't know. It's not as if we intended to hide her away. It began with her not wanting to face people. She was like this tender, wounded flower. She was happy as long as she was in her own familiar surroundings. But take her out among people and she closed up, seemed to wither before our eyes.

"And people can be so cruel. She couldn't bear the stares and thoughtless remarks. So Mother and I gave in and let her keep to herself. At the time it seemed the kindest thing to humor her, let her have her own way, her isolation. Frankly, we got caught up in it ourselves. Mother and I tried to create a fantasy world for her where she could be happy in spite of her handicaps. And after a while it seemed easier not to mention Belina than to have people wonder why she stayed hidden away in her room."

"But she never had a chance to grow emotionally, Antonio, or to test her abilities physically. Even her room reflects her arrested development. It's the room of a little girl, not a grown woman."

"I see that now, Cassandra, but I was blind to it before. You've got to understand, I had my own devils to fight. My mother and I were as much prisoners as Belina. We were all captives." He lowered his head and rubbed his temples, as if to diffuse a terrible pounding in his skull. When he looked back at Cassie, his eyes were red-rimmed. "Don't you see? I didn't want to witness Belina's pain and humiliation around other people because it reminded me of my own guilt."

"Your guilt? You mean the accident?"

"Yes. Since I was a boy I have blamed myself for my father's death and my sister's injuries." Antonio's jaw tightened. "I felt I had to atone for my sins. I had to be the best at whatever I did. The best performer…the model brother…the model son. I had no time for a personal life…a wife…children. I vowed I would live my entire life taking care of my mother and sister, because I had robbed them of so much."

"But you didn't, Antonio!" Cassie protested. "It was your father who robbed all of you of a happy family. You were the victim as much as anyone."

"I see that now. Since knowing you, and since talking with your father these last few days, many things are clearer to me." Antonio reached across the table and took Cassie's hand between his palms. His touch was warm, electrifying. "You have helped me see so many things, Cassandra. Some things I didn't wish to see. At first I was angry with you because you thought the worst of me. But more than that, I was angry because you made me face the truth about myself. I have been as much a coward as Belina, refusing to face the real world, afraid to risk loving someone, afraid even to let God open up a new life to me. But you have helped set me free. God has used you and your father to help me and my mother and sister break free from the past."

"I'm so glad you feel that way, Antonio." Cassie bit her lower lip to keep back the tears. "I was sick inside, thinking I had harmed your family, that my actions might have contributed to your sister's fall down the stairs."

"Then you have a little taste of the guilt I have lived with." He locked his fingers with hers and squeezed so tightly she almost winced. "But enough talk of the past. I have something else to say."

"I hope you're going to tell me we can still be friends."

He rubbed his chin with his free hand, as if debating the question. "Friends? I don't know about that."

"But you just said—"

"I said I am very grateful to you, but that doesn't mean I want us to be friends."

With sudden indignation, Cassie tugged at her hand, trying to untangle her fingers from Antonio's. She wasn't about to hold hands with a man who didn't even want to be friends.

"Wait, my dear Cassandra. I'm not finished!" He leaned across the table, his face close enough that she could smell the coffee on his warm breath. His dark eyes twinkled merrily. "I don't want to be friends, my darling. I want to be so much more."

She stared at him, transfixed. "More?"

He glanced around the noisy, drab cafeteria and smiled grimly. "This isn't exactly the setting I would have chosen. Pretend we're sitting on the beach in the moonlight."

"I don't want to pretend anything, Antonio. I just want to know what you're trying to tell me."

He massaged her hand, one finger at a time. "I'm trying to say…I finished the song I was writing. Remember? The song about you? The little ditty that would make Longfellow cringe?"

She smiled. "Come now, Antonio. Don't belittle your poetic genius. I loved your little song."

"Well, for weeks I couldn't come up with the last verse. But now I have. Last night I stayed up for hours thinking and praying, praying and thinking, trying to resolve all the complications in my life.''

He paused to kiss each of Cassie's fingertips, then went on in a half whisper. ''I kept picturing you with Drake Cameron and kicking myself because I hadn't stopped you from seeing him. And suddenly, as I prayed, all the puzzle pieces seemed to fall into place, and I could see the whole picture. And it was almost as if God were saying, 'Wake up, Antonio! Cassandra's the woman I chose for you. What are you waiting for? Get off your duff, or you'll lose her!' ''

Cassie burst out laughing. ''I can't imagine God using the word *duff!*''

''Nor can I. But that's how it translated in my head.''

''But what does the song you wrote have to do with—''

''Let me finish.'' He gave her a sly, mysterious grin. ''I'm going to sing the song for you, Cassandra.''

She looked around in alarm. ''Not here, with all the noise, and the doctors and nurses milling about, and all these people staring at us!''

''No, of course not!''

''Then where?''

He leaned closer, his face mere inches from hers, and whispered in her ear, ''At our wedding. I'll sing the song for you at our wedding. You will be there, won't you?''

Cassie's head spun, and her heart fluttered like

butterflies being set free. "Our wedding? Antonio, is this a proposal?"

His smile made her heart leap. "Darling, I'd get down on one knee, but some doctor would probably think I'd fallen and needed attention, and they'd cart me off to the emergency room, kicking and screaming."

She laughed again. "Silly, they would not!"

His lips curled seductively. "But if you don't want me to make a spectacle of myself, I suggest you give me an answer."

She moved forward, as close as the table between them would allow, and avowed, "Yes, Antonio, I'll be at your wedding. I wouldn't miss it for the world. Now do I get to hear my song?"

"I'll whisper the last verse for your ears alone. 'Cassandra, my Cassandra, I take you for my wife. I'll cherish and affirm you and love you all my life. Cassandra, my Cassandra, may God bless our happy home, and keep us in His will wherever we may roam.'"

Cassie pressed her fingertips to her trembling lips. "I love it, Antonio. I love *you!*"

His mahogany eyes crinkled with unabashed delight. "Are you saying you'll be my bride?"

She nodded, matching his smile. "Your bride...your wife...your helpmate...and the mother of your children."

Amid a throng of doctors, nurses, attendants and visitors and patients consuming sausages and doughnuts and coffee in a whitewashed, utilitarian room smelling of medicine and crowded with orange plas-

tic tables with tubular legs…Antonio stood to his full
height and bowed with the rakish gallantry of a
prince, and swept Cassandra into his arms and kissed
her with unbridled passion, for all the world to see.

It was a priceless, jubilant, hilarious memory that
Cassie would carry in her heart until she and her
ravishing husband were ancient and gray.

Epilogue

The Reverend Andrew Rowlands
and Mrs. Juliana Pagliarulo
joyfully invite you to the wedding of their children
Cassandra Rowlands and Antonio Pagliarulo
at the Cornerstone Christian Church of La Jolla
Saturday, June 23rd at 2:00 p.m.
The Reverend Andrew Rowlands Officiating
Reception Immediately Following

Andrew had never seen his daughter Cassie look lovelier. As she swished across the church vestibule in her satin-and-lace gown, a flowing veil lending a gossamer sheen to her upswept, silky blond hair, he was convinced no princess could rival her beauty. And within minutes, she would march down the aisle to her Prince Charming, the debonair Antonio Pagliarulo.

Even as he watched Cassie giving her sisters last-minute instructions, Andrew mused that events couldn't have gone better if he had orchestrated them himself. His oldest daughter was finally marrying the man of her dreams, an honorable, godly man, with faults to be sure, like everyone else. But oh, how Antonio loved Cassie! Yes, indeed, they would be good for each other.

Already they were considering ways they could combine their music as a ministry in churches around the country. What a team they made! Praise God, they had the Master Planner in their lives, guiding them, helping them become the people He wanted them to be.

And surely someday they would bring home a little bundle of sunshine, mused Andrew, a precious baby, his first grandchild to kiss and cuddle and bounce on his knee. Maybe it would be a sweet little girl like Cassie, and he would have to start thinking about the men who would come into her life someday.

But if his daughter's romance had been orchestrated by the Almighty, why was there so much bedlam in the vestibule now as his three daughters— two bridesmaids and one bride—scurried around, preparing to walk down the aisle? Where was the quiet serenity of this moment, the dignity, the grandeur?

His youngest daughter Frannie jarred his tranquility with, "Cassie! Cassie, where's the garter?" Like his middle daughter Brianna, Frannie was wearing a simple but elegant rose-colored, ankle-length bridesmaid dress. "Do you hear me, Cassie? I can't find the garter!"

"Calm down, Fran! It's already on my leg," Cassie replied, pulling up her crinolines to expose a powder-blue garter on her shapely leg.

"What about something borrowed, something blue?" cried Bree.

"The garter's blue," said Cassie, "and I borrowed your diamond earrings, Bree."

"You did? Oh, yeah, I thought they looked familiar."

"You don't mind?"

"Not today."

"Do I look okay? Is anything showing that's not supposed to show?"

"No, and what does show looks fantastic," said Frannie.

This was Andrew's cue. Feeling pleasantly urbane in his black tuxedo, he strode over to Cassie and took her small, nervous hands in his. "Baby doll, you look absolutely radiant. Ah, my darling, if only your mother could see you now! Magnificent! I will be so proud to walk you down the aisle."

Cassie's ivory cheeks flushed with roses. "Thanks, Daddy. I'm so glad to have you walking with me."

Frannie slipped over and nudged her father playfully. "One down, two to go, right, Daddy?"

Andrew pinched Frannie's cheek. "Maybe so, cupcake, but who's counting?"

"You are," said Bree. "You would have been delighted to make this a triple wedding."

"How about a quadruple, Daddy?" teased Cassie. "There's still Juliana."

Andrew nodded. "And a fine woman she is. Who knows? If there's ever another lady in my life, Juliana it will be. And maybe someday…"

"Better not let her get snatched up by some other man," warned Bree. "She's not going to wait around forever, you know."

Andrew grinned. "Now, my darling daughters, don't worry about Juliana and me. We have an understanding. Neither of us is ready to make any major changes in our lives just yet. She still has Belina to look after, and I still have my two girls at home."

Frannie tweaked his cheek. "But not for long, if you can help it, right, Daddy?"

"No way, baby cakes. My matchmaking days are over!" He glanced at his watch. "Say, isn't it time to get this show on the road? Everyone is seated and I hear the organ playing."

Cassie looked around. "Where's Juliana?"

"She's still in the dressing room with Belina," said Bree.

Andrew gave Cassie a quizzical glance. "Do you think this is going to work? Belina's still awfully skittish around crowds."

"We told her anytime she feels uncomfortable, Juliana will take her back to the dressing room."

Andrew scratched his head. "Well, this is going to be one whopper of a surprise for Antonio."

"I can't wait to see his face," said Cassie, her own countenance glowing. "Now if Juliana would just hurry!"

"Did someone mention my name?" Juliana bustled up beside Andrew and squeezed his arm. She looked marvelous in a bright-pink knit suit. "We're ready if you are, Cassandra."

Andrew let his gaze move past Juliana to the frail slip of a girl standing behind her. Belina looked positively angelic in her shimmery, pale-rose bridesmaid dress. Her shiny black hair hung in gentle waves to her shoulders and a gold tiara graced the top of her head. She balanced herself with two canes.

Andrew went over and kissed her forehead. "Belina, you look like a story-book princess."

She blushed. "I—I've never been so scared in my life."

"You'll do just fine," he assured her. "Brianna and Frannie will march down the aisle first, then you and your mom, then Cassie and me."

"You make it sound so simple."

"No, not simple, Belina. But you've been working toward this day for months. And, remember, you're surrounded by love."

Juliana stole over and tucked her daughter's arm in hers. "Belina, when your brother sees you walking down the aisle by yourself, he will be so excited, so pleased. You couldn't give him a better wedding present."

Cassie swept over, holding her voluminous gown off the floor, and gave Belina a gentle hug. "Your being in our wedding is the best present either of us could receive."

Belina smiled, her white-cream face blossoming

with color. "I haven't let Tonio know how well I'm walking. I wanted to surprise him."

"He will be stunned, jubilant," Cassie said. "In fact, he may not even notice me coming down the aisle when he sees you."

"No, Cassie. I know my brother. He only has eyes for you."

Andrew slipped his arm around Cassie's shoulder. "If I'm not mistaken, that's the Wedding March. It's time to begin."

Cassie gazed up at her father with luminous eyes. "It is a beginning, isn't it, Daddy? A wonderful new beginning for all of us. How I wish Mother could be here with us!"

"Me, too, baby girl." Andrew felt a sudden catch in his throat. "But I have a feeling she's watching from her own balcony seat in glory and showering us with her love."

As Juliana and Belina assumed their position in the procession line behind his two younger daughters, Andrew took his place beside Cassie. She was already gazing blissfully down the aisle to the altar where Antonio stood waiting.

Andrew smiled inwardly. Yes, all was well that ended well, and this had certainly ended better than he expected. He had to give the Lord credit for that, of course. God had a way of working through his bumbling children to produce great results.

Well, Lord, he mused silently as he escorted Cassie down the aisle, the two marching in measured cadence and exchanging private smiles, *You say we have not because we ask not. Well, I'm asking, Lord, because I'm a man who knows his frailties. I know I need lots of help. I've got two lovely daughters who still need husbands. What do You think we can do about them, Lord?*

*   *   *   *   *

Dear Reader,

I hope you enjoyed reading about Reverend Rowlands and his three plucky, matchmaking daughters as much as I enjoyed writing about them. My goal was to create in Andrew Rowlands the sort of loving, affirming father every young girl dreams of—a totally devoted daddy you can turn to and trust and know he'll be there for you, no matter what.

A little bit like our Heavenly Father, who loves us unconditionally and wants to be there for us through all the ups and downs of our lives, who cherishes us with a "great and wonderful and intense love" beyond anything we can imagine.

What fun I had portraying two tender, unpredictable romances in one Love Inspired novel—Andrew's budding affection for the exquisite Juliana Pagliarulo as well as Cassandra's igniting ardor for Juliana's handsome, enigmatic son, Antonio. I chose an Italian heritage for Juliana and Antonio because my husband, Bill, is half-Italian.

But a third romance weaves its way through my book, and that's the most important one of all. I tried to capture the joy and passionate abandon we can experience in the presence of our Savior when we pour out our love for Him and experience His limitless love in return.

Dear friend, if only we could comprehend how much the Savior loves us! May His love warm our hearts, renew our strength and inspire us to new heights of joy and delight.

I'd love to hear from you. Let me know what you think of the Rowlands clan. Write me c/o Steeple Hill Books, 300 East 42nd Street, New York, New York 10017. And be sure to watch for the romantic adventures of Andrew's next two daughters...as well as Andrew's continuing romance with the enchanting Juliana.

Celebrating our Father's love,

Carole Gift Page